Hemanter Pakhi

Autumn Bird

Hemanter Pakhi

Autumn Bird

Suchitra Bhattacharya

Translated by
Swapna Dutta

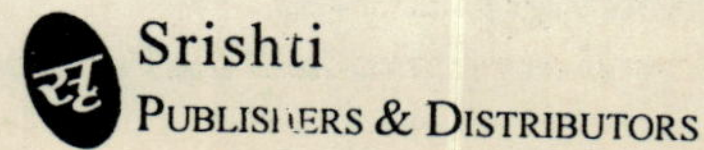
Srishti
Publishers & Distributors

SRISHTI PUBLISHERS & DISTRIBUTORS
64-A, Adhchini
Sri Aurobindo Marg
New Delhi 110 017
srishtipublishers@forindia.com
srishtipublishers@yahoo.com

First published in English by SRISHTI PUBLISHERS & DISTRIBUTORS in 2003

ISBN 81-88575-03-8
Rs. 195.00

Cover design: Vinayak Bhattacharya
Cover photographs: Courtesy NFDC

Typeset in AGaramond 11pt. by Skumar at Srishti

Printed and bound in India by
Saurabh Print-O-Pack, Noida

Chapter One

Aditi was trying to make the caged parrot talk. It was something she tried every afternoon when there was no one around. The parrot was determined not to utter a sound. Aditi was equally determined to get her way. It was a strange game involving the two.

Aditi had bought the bird a couple of months ago from a wayside dealer, paying eighty rupees in hard cash. The bird wasn't particularly young. In fact, it was fairly big in size. Its deep green colour looked mature, as did its well grown wings and the clear black buckle – like a band around its neck. The bird-seller had held forth about its many virtues. He could have beaten Supratim, the seasoned salesman, hollow!

"Take the bird, Boudi" he had pleaded, "It's fully trained and just ready for a home. You'd need less than a week to tame it – totally and absolutely. Can't you see it's a genuine Singapore parrot? It'll chatter nineteen to the dozen and repeat whatever it gets to hear. Stretch out your arms and it will fly to you. It will cling to your shoulder like a baby. In fact, you won't even feel like putting it inside a cage, you'll get so fond of it."

But the bird refused to talk. For more than a month now Aditi had heard nothing more than a harsh, ugly croak from it. As for taming the creature, the bird came to attack her with a raucous squawk even when she tried to feed it. It was downright humiliating! Something that made her feel embarrassed before Supratim and her two sons.

All three felt the same about the parrot. It was old. Old and totally useless.

But Aditi found it hard to accept it.

Perhaps the bird was actually bright, sharp, and intelligent.

Perhaps it refused to talk because it expected her to feel exasperated and open the door of the cage some day. That would set it free to streak across the sky once more.

Perhaps it just couldn't forget the trees and the rivers, the forest and the open sky it had left behind.

And perhaps it was determined not to talk unless those memories were wiped clean from its consciousness.

But that didn't mean that Aditi should give up trying.

Even Papai, her son, had been weak in mathematics when he was a child. He couldn't even manage simple multiplications and divisions. He chewed up his pencils to a pulp, trying to solve them.

He'd mutter, "I don't understand it, Mom" or "I can't manage it Mom", or "Mom, it's totally beyond me".

But Aditi hadn't given up trying. And now mathematics was his strong point.

He had scored ninety-seven percent in his Secondary exams, and hundred and ninety in his Higher Secondary. He'd won prizes at inter-school mathematics competitions. So many of them! Now that he was in the third year of college his classmates sought his help in solving tough problems in physics. Surely making a bird talk couldn't be tougher than what she had gone through to make him lose his fear of mathematics?

Aditi gently shook the iron cage that hung from a rod in her balcony.

"Well?" she asked in a low voice, "Won't you really speak – ever?"

The parrot fluttered across to the other side.

Aditi followed it and pressed her face against the cage.

"Come on, speak. Say 'Supratim'. S-u-p-r-a-t-i-m. Say it, say it, I tell you!"

But the parrot couldn't be bothered uttering a word with so many syllables. It turned its neck looking disdainfully at Aditi and moved away once again.

"I understand" she muttered, "You don't like my hubby, do you? That's why you won't say it. It's natural; he doesn't like you either."

The parrot remained dumb; it seemed to agree with what was being said.

Aditi smiled. "Very well, call Papai and Tatai, then. Say P-a-p-a-i! T-a-t-a-i!"

The parrot made anther croaking sound and plonked itself down on the floor of the cage. Then it started fluttering around.

"You really are a boor! Can't you at least call your brothers?"

The parrot flew up at the top of the cage and swung like a gymnast.

"Very well, then. You don't have to call anyone else. Just call me. Say Aditi. A-d-i-t-i!"

The parrot jumped back on its perch and started blinking, over and over again.

"Don't tell me you find even Aditi difficult to pronounce?" she said in a whisper. "Do you want something simpler? Very well. Say Khuku. K-h-u-k-u."

Both her sons used to call her Khuku when they were young. It was Supratim who taught them to call her that. The younger one continued to call her by that name for a long time. Tatai called her Khuku-ma even when he was in class five. How she used to scold him for doing it!

She couldn't imagine why she felt a sudden craving to hear the old name once again after all these years!

She sighed and made a last attempt. "Won't you call me Khuku-ma just once? Come on! Say it."

The parrot screeched loudly.

"Why are you screeching, you rascal?"

The parrot screeched once again.

"It's useless trying to teach you anything. The others knew it from the start that you're far too old to learn anything – Old and senile."

Aditi walked away from the cage and stared at it from afar. So the birdman had really cheated her, taking all that money for a bird that was no good!

But there was nothing unexpected about her being cheated. Shortly before buying the parrot she had fallen for a mynah from Nepal and had bought it instantly. She'd stand before the cage for hours, waiting to hear it speak. But as luck would have it, the bird merely stuffed itself silly and messed up the cage. Nothing more! It flew away one fine morning finding the cage door open.

How Supratim and her sons jeered at her when it happened. They insisted that it was a magpie and not a mynah at all. It was just like Aditi to have mistaken it for one!

Perhaps they were right.

Another time when Papai and Tatai were very young she had bought some lovebirds from a fair. They made a gorgeous riot of colour – green and yellow, black, blue and brown. But as soon as her sons sprayed them with a syringe, trying to give them a bath, their colours ran out and they turned out to be a pack of sparrows.

Supratim had been wild with her for having wasted thirty rupees on the birds.

"I can't really expect you to understand the value of money since you don't have to earn any," he had told her in a taunting voice. But things were different now. Supratim was no longer bothered about her wasting such a meagre amount. He was not a mere salesman now, always having to rush around; he was the high and mighty area manager of Lotus India.

Aditi stared at the parrot for a while and went inside the room.

Malina's mother, her maid, had left the washed clothes piled up on her bed. Aditi folded them up neatly and sorted them into different piles. Shorts and T-shirts belonging to her sons in one, Supratim's vests and undies in another, her own saris, slips, and blouses in a third. She put away each pile where it belonged – cupboards, racks, her own room and that of her sons.

Then she stretched on the bed, re-read the old newspaper, turning its pages once again. Finally she pushed it aside and closed her eyes. It was not easy to fall asleep when she wasn't sleepy. And she didn't want to, either. Sleeping in the afternoon would merely bring on an attack of acidity and make her feel queasy all evening. That's how it was these days, ever since her last surgery.

Would she try teaching the parrot some more or just lie down and take it easy? Why not try knitting something? But what was the use! Her sons preferred machine-knit sweaters any day.

What was she to do? How could she fill up the void that looked like an endless stretch of time?

It was now late autumn.

There was something magical about this period stretching between early autumn and winter. It seemed to appear out of the blue, its face covered in a veil of mist and having appeared, it seemed to go on forever and ever. The breeze turned dry, the skin stretched uncomfortably as one heard the footsteps of winter in the distance. And yet winter did not quite set in. The breeze continued to smell of autumn. It was a strange, inactive span between lively autumn and freezing winter – dawdling and lethargic.

The telephone rang. Aditi stood up. Then she ambled down to the drawing space with lazy steps and picked up the phone unhurriedly. It was Supratim calling.

"What's up? Were you asleep?"

"Not quite ... just a little ..."

"That's like you! That's what happens when one has no worries"

"Did you call me just to tell me that?"

"You sound annoyed. Is it because I interrupted your siesta?"

Aditi smiled. "Why don't you come to the point?"

Did Supratim sound a trifle hesitant? Perhaps not. Finally he stated his reason for calling.

"Have I left a pink file at home by mistake? Just check if it is lying on the table of our bedroom."

"Hang on, I'll just go and see," Aditi said, rushing to the bedroom.

"Yes, it's here."

"Thanks be! I was afraid I'd left it behind in the taxi. It's chockfull of important documents."

"Didn't you carry your briefcase this morning?"

"Haven't you noticed that I've not been carrying it for quite some time now?"

Aditi could have answered that she hadn't. Where was the time to notice such trivial things in the mornings? All her time was fully taken up by Papai and Tatai. That was the only time they still needed her.

"Mom, please press my trousers."

"There's a button off my shirt – sew it on, quick!"

"Oh Lord, why have you piled up so much rice on my plate? Take it away – fast!"

In between all these demands Aditi somehow managed to leave Supratim's tie, socks and handkerchief on the bed. But she no longer had the time to see him off at the door. Not for a long, long time.

Aditi changed the subject lightly.

"Why did you remember the file after four long hours if it's all that important?"

"That's something you're not likely to understand," came the prompt reply, "You've never had to work so you don't know what it's like. For you, life has merely been one long stretch of leisure. I was busy with a meeting with the sales people right from the first hour. I could remember the file only when I had a breather."

"I see."

Aditi's next question was a futile one.

"When do you expect to be back?"

"Me? Do you mean this evening?" Supratim could not conceal the surprise in his voice. "As usual, I expect. Around nine thirty or ten. Our agent from Patna is here. I'll need to sit with him for a while."

"Don't drink too much. And don't forget about your high blood pressure."

"I won't. Don't preach, for goodness' sake."

"I wouldn't if I didn't know that you completely lose your head the moment you see a bottle. Are you going to have your dinner at home tonight or waste all the food like you did last night?"

"Of course I'll dine at home. I'm not going out for an official dinner tonight. So long!"

The line snapped dead marking the end of their conjugal tete a tete.

Aditi held on to the receiver for a while turning it around

for a few seconds or more. When time hung heavy even the few seconds seemed endless. The tiny flat of seven hundred square feet, chock a block with furniture, felt like an unending realm of wilderness.

The receiver in her hand was beginning to hum. Like an appeal that muttered 'put me back, put me back'. Aditi wiped it once more and put it back on its cradle.

The instrument had been part of her household for the last three years. But Supratim merely used it for passing on information. He'd never ever used it to whisper sweet nothings!

Aditi often wondered what he'd have done if they had a telephone when they were first married. Would he have called her up at noon and spoken to her in such a matter of fact voice? Surely not!

Supratim used to be quite different in those days. He had both care and concern for her. He used to call her by such a soft, sweet name – Phool, flower.

Phool. He still called her that sometimes. But he meant a fool and not a flower.

Aditi started dusting the sofa absent-mindedly. Malina's mother had made an attempt to dust carefully but Aditi was not satisfied with her work. She seemed to find imaginary specks of dust all over the place. On the cabinet, on the centre table, on the TV screen – everywhere.

Did it signify an excessive attachment to her home?

She sat quietly on the sofa for a while. Then she got up and switched on the TV. And sat down once again. It was no fun watching TV alone, all by herself. No sense gaping at the series of moving figures – laughing, crying, singing, making love or bumping someone off as she watched them passively. She felt like an idiot doing it. It was all so false. She just could not identify with the figures on the screen. They seemed like mere moving puppets. And it made her feel like one when she sat down to watch them. What was the use of watching something if there was no one to share it with? She didn't mind watching a cricket or a tennis match all day long, along with Papai or Tatai. But not just by herself.

Her afternoons used to be so different even two or three years ago. Until he passed his Secondary Board exams Tatai attended morning school. The entire house would hum with activity all day long. Tatai slamming the bathroom door shut. Tatai singing at the top of his voice. Tatai turning on the TV at full volume. Tatai playing taped music full blast. Tatai shouting questions all day long.

"Mom, what have you done to my Brian Adams cassette?"

"Mom, Papai has worn my T-shirt again! Why didn't you forbid him?"

"Mom, there's a cold drink in the fridge, may I have it?"

"Oh dear, where's my Walkman? Mom, please find it for me."

It was Mom, Mom, Mom and Mom all day long.

She used to find it too noisy at the time.

But now that he was no longer there to call her everything seemed to be breathlessly quiet and empty.

But all said and done, Tatai was still childish in some ways. He still threw his arms round her as he asked for this or that. But Papai already felt like a grown up.

The same Papai who used to dote on her even five years ago.

He'd tell her every single thing – from school tutorials, to games, friends and all. He'd chatter about all and sundry whether she wanted to listen to him or not. And now he hardly ever opened his mouth at home. Her sons had found their own circles. Or grown their wings, perhaps?

Papai and Tatai were flying away from her, that much was certain. They would come back to their nest sometime, no doubt.

But fly away again ... and again ... since the entire blue sky stretched out before them invitingly.

And Aditi had her flat. It felt like a limitless empty stretch of 700 square feet.

Aditi's eyes were glued to the TV screen. It showed a film song, possibly a very old one. But she could neither see it nor hear it. It was a quarter to three. Malina's mother would arrive around four to do the dishes. Sabita, the cook would land up half an hour later to cook dinner. The boys might return home early or they might not. It was quite useless to prepare snacks for them in advance. She'd rustle up something if and when they landed up. There were some boiled peas, she'd use those for preparing a quick snack.

She remembered that she'd have to make a trip to the Daspara market. Papai had to see his tutor in the morning . He wouldn't be able to do her shopping. That meant her having to buy the fish and vegetables tonight. She'd have to buy a tube of toothpaste and some soap as well. Of course all these things were also available in the shop across the road. Supratim had mentioned new shoe-laces. Would those be available at Daspara, she wondered. She'd have to get fresh grams for the bird too. Its bowl was empty. She'd need to soak fresh ones.

Something seemed to prick her inside the moment she thought of the bird and how she'd been cheated. Why did a person cheat another for the sake of a small amount? She could have made a gift of the money to the bird-seller had he but asked for it. She had done it so many times in the past. Hadn't she given fifty rupees to the ironing man at the corner for buying medicine? Had she asked him to return the money? She never would unless he volunteered to return it himself. Well ... let it be, she thought. Let them cheat her. She spent so much of her time with the bird. Wasn't that a kind of payment too?

Aditi walked up to the bird again. It seemed to be listening to something, bending its head to catch the sounds. Was it listening to the music blared out by the television? Her heart leaped up at the thought. What had the birdman told her at the time of selling it? "Keep the TV on quite loudly. The bird will hear it and learn to whistle."

Well she didn't need the TV to teach the bird to whistle. She could whistle very well herself. She had so often put her sons to sleep whistling tunes.

But could she do it now? She hadn't done it for years!

She pointed her lips and breathed out air. Why, she could still whistle as well as ever! Perhaps one never forgot how to whistle just as one never forgot how to cycle or swim.

Aditi closed the TV and returned to the in balcony. She carefully looked around at the other flats nearby. There were three others in the same complex. They seemed to be dozing in the sweet and refreshing sun of autumn. Not a soul was in sight in any of the balconies. Oh yes, there was someone. On the fourth floor of the flat opposite hers. It was Shipra's old mother-in-law. The old woman could neither see nor hear properly. But she remained glued to the balcony despite that. Why did she do it? Just to smell the sunlight and the fresh air?

Aditi went close to the cage and whistled softly.

The parrot gave a start and looked up.

Aditi whistled again; a prolonged one this time.

The parrot tilted its head a little. Was it listening? Its read beaks seemed to quiver just a little. The sight cheered her up immensely. She whistled again and again.

The parrot started and looked at her every time.

Aditi turned the sheer blowing of air into a proper tune. And rhyme. She was still able to do it pretty well.

Whistling popular tunes of film songs had been no big deal for her during her college days. She could even whistle the theme tune of *The Bridge on the River Kwai*. She had whistled it for Supratim during their honeymoon in Puri as they sat side by side on the beach, facing the breakers. The musical notes of her whistle seemed to sway with the waves. Supratim was charmed... enchanted! He could never have imagined a bride whistling ... whistling a tune that was good enough for listening to. He tried it himself but the feat was beyond him. His thick lips could only blow out air. Aditi had burst out laughing at his efforts. A beaten and embarrassed Supratim had thrown his arms round her and pleaded with her to do it once more, and yet once more. It must have driven him crazy or could he have asked a newly wed bride to whistle in bed? Aditi, eager to tease him had let out a shrill catcall that she had picked up from a naughty friend. A real shrill catcall! Supratim started in surprise knocking off the glass vase on the table breaking it into fragments. The South Indian family in the next room – father, mother and two children – had stared at them the next morning. Possibly they had thought that this was the Bengali way of making love!

Should she try that same wild catcall once again? Who was there to hear it? There wasn't a soul for miles around. She turned her back to Shipra's mother-in-law and put her finger under her tongue. But something made her stop. What was the point in giving vent to such childishness? The apartments were teeming with people. Someone might hear her without her being aware of it.

She remembered another craze that had taken hold of her a few months back. She would sit before her dressing table the moment her flat was empty and slap on layers of cream, powder and lipstick on her face and lips. Not content with painting her face she would wear Supratim's shirt and trousers and walk about the entire place like a model on a catwalk. She'd try stepping like a cat, a lion or a deer. One day some noise outside had brought her to the balcony and she had looked down. That was when everyone got to know about her stupidity. She had screamed herself hoarse telling her family that it was all a big mistake and that people had seen someone else, not her.

If someone were to hear her catcalling now and spread the word around, she was sure Papai and Tatai would dump her, their 45-year-old mother, in the mental asylum at Ranchi. Aditi could see herself roaming about all by herself in the streets of Ranchi, asking people where the asylum was. She could also see the passers-by running for their lives at her question while she chased them relentlessly. The entire scene seemed so hilarious that she burst out laughing. She was still laughing as she crept inside the room. She continued to laugh as she lay in bed... laughed and laughed until her jaws ached along with her tummy ... and her lips remained open in a cheesy grin. When at last she stopped the same old problem returned. Time seemed to stand still once again.

She pulled out a magazine from the side table, a much-read one that she practically knew by heart. But she turned the pages, nevertheless. Then she threw it down, got up and went to the room shared by her sons. Fumbling among the books on Papai's table she picked up a thick book. A thriller in English that had a half naked woman and a machine gun on the cover. The back cover carried the synopsis of the story. Aditi glanced at the lines, made a face and put it down. Finally she took a Bengali book out of the bookcase. That was an oft-read one too. So were all the other books. How many times could one read and re-read the same old ones? If only there had been a library in the locality! There used to be such a nice one near their place in Zamir Lane where she had lived with her in-laws. Her father-in-law would get new ones as soon as she finished reading the books. Aditi virtually gobbled up the new books as she sat with her baby in her arms.

Aditi's eyes fell on the line of ants climbing up her wall. Every one of them carried a speck of white in its mouth. A well organized journey, possibly preparing for the winter. The line moved from floor to ceiling. Not a straight line, nor a crooked one. It looked more like a strand of black thread suspended on the wall, shaking a little and dispersing on all sides after reaching the ceiling in a wonderful geometrical pattern.

Suddenly there came the sound of the doorbell ringing. Probably it was Malin's mother come to work. As she opened the door Aditi stared in surprise at the oldish man, slightly bent, who stood at the door. He wore a kurta and pyjama. He had a cotton shawl on his shoulder and a long-handled umbrella in one hand. He was smiling at her. He looked vaguely familiar. Who could it be? His eyes laughed behind the glasses and spread across his sunken cheeks.

"Can't you recognize me?"

Aditi knew him the moment he spoke. It was his baritone voice that told her who he was.

"Hemen Mama, isn't it?" she said.

Chapter Two

"You know, I had a visitor today" said Aditi as they sat dining that night.

"Who was it?" asked Supratim, busy spreading onion slices on the gram-curry. He did not lift his head from the bowl.

"Hemen Mama"

"Hemen who?"

Supratim frowned as he looked at his sons. "Stop making such a racket, for goodness' sake! Can't you live without squabbling at the dinner table every single night?"

The brothers were arguing about cricket. The Indian team was going abroad for a match and the names of the players had just been announced. Tatai didn't approve of the choice. A fresher in college, Tatai considered himself a virtual know-all. But Papai, who was two years older than him, still thought him a kid and dismissed his views as baby talk. He never lost his cool in an argument but his trite comments put Tatai in a royal rage.

Tatai didn't hear his father's words and shouted, "Don't talk like a fool! You never even got the chance to play in a school match so how can you possibly pretend to know everything?"

"I understand the game, nevertheless" replied Papai and turning a serious face towards his father, said, "Did you hear him call me a fool, Dad?"

Supratim raised his voice. "Tatai, if you can't speak politely, don't get into arguments with your brother."

"I can't help it if he persists on making idiotic comments. A player who couldn't make a name for himself despite playing in 14 Test Matches ...."

"Look, Dad, he is calling me an idiot now" said Papai concentrating on his food.

"For goodness' sake shut up, Tatai, and let people eat in peace" remarked Aditi giving him a bowl of chicken curry. "What sort of people do you mix with these days? You are beginning to sound like a boor!"

Tatai ground his teeth but decided to hold his tongue. He was no match for his brother and had no aptitude for the kind of subtle tricks he used to get the better of an argument. He merely shouted at the top of his voice and ended up having to eat his own words. It was quite usual for him to lose an argument and leave the table in a huff without having his meal.

As he lifted his hand from the bowl Aditi smiled and ruffled his hair. "Come on finish your food."

Supratim gave him an angry look and said, " Let him be. Don't spoil him. Who did you say your visitor was?"

Aditi, after having served everyone, was eating now. She spooned some grams in her mouth and replied, "Hemen Mama. A friend of my youngest uncle. He used to visit our house at Amherst Street quite often. He is a writer."

Papai looked up. "What's his full name?"

Aditi thought for a moment and replied, "Hemendra Narayan Mullick"

"Never heard of him!"

"Do you know the names of each and every writer?" protested Tatai in a sneering voice, "I have read three novels by one Hemendra Mullick – can't remember his middle name, though."

"You reading novels! That too in Bengali! That's a good one!"

"Ah Tatai, stop it, will you?" said Aditi exasperated. Turning to Supratim she said, "By writer I didn't exactly mean a particularly famous one. He wrote a great deal, that's all. He had been to uncle's place recently and got my address from him."

"But what made him look you up all of a sudden?"

"No particular reason. Just like that" said Aditi in an embarrassed voice, "I used to write quite a lot myself once upon a time. He used to be very fond of me."

"You writing?" asked Tatai in round-eyed astonishment, quite forgetting his anger.

"Of course I did! Our school magazines carried so many of my poems. Our college magazine brought out a story by me. Annapurnadidi, our Bengali professor, praised it to the skies. Ask your father if you don't believe me."

"How on earth should I know anything about it?" Supratim sounded astonished.

"Don't pretend! I told you myself soon after we were married. And why just me, both my father and my mother told you about my writing."

"People say a lot of things when a girl is about to be married. One has to take it with a pinch of salt." Supratim winked at the boys. "Don't you remember how your mother had said that you were a fabulous cook when it came to non-vegetarian dishes? And what did you do when you had to cook meat for the first time at our place? Turned out an over-salted hash! It was just as well that my father didn't have the heart to hurt a bride so he washed the meat pieces in water and gulped it down somehow!"

"How could you compare cooking to something like writing?" asked Aditi in a hurt voice.

"It's all the same. Both need spicing up. People chew some and gulp some."

"It's no use expecting you to understand! Have you ever

read a single book just for the fun of it? Those who love to read know how difficult it is to write. Do you know what Hemen Mama told me today? He said – "You wrote so well once ... have you really given it up?"

"Why all this regret? Write all you want to! What's stopping you?"

"Yes, Mom write an autobiography. Memoirs of a housewife" Papai interjected, "We'll arrange about the publication if you're able to complete it."

Tatai was still smarting. "Who's going to publish it? You?"

"Not me. But Dad will. Dad, would you mind spending eight or ten grand to publish Mom's book? I'm sure she'll write many nice things about you in her memoir."

Supratim burst out laughing. "Eight or ten thousand isn't a big sum. Have you any idea how many thousands your mother blew up trying her hand at setting up a sari business? A solid sixteen thousand!"

Aditi tried to protest. "Didn't I return you some of it?"

"That's precisely why I said sixteen thousand. If you hadn't, I'd have said twenty," remarked Supratim picking out pieces from a chicken bone.

Aditi held her tongue.

Really how could she have been so crazy! She wanted to try her hand at business because time hung heavy and she didn't know what to do with herself. Supratim had offered to give her the capital. No harm if she managed to earn something by doing something practical. So Aditi had roamed around Bara Bazar buying saris at wholesale rates and sold them to people she knew, taking her payment in instalments. She was supposed to keep a profit of twenty percent for herself.

But she was just not cut out for the job. She blurted out the actual price without thinking and then had to lower her price accordingly. Instead of taking the payment in three instalments she ended up taking it in six or eight. Even then she felt embarrassed to ask for payment and felt like a professional moneylender! Some relatives had really exploited the situation, telling her, "Khuku, it's ages since you've given me a gift during the pujas. I'm keeping this sari as one." Another one said, "How much was I supposed to pay you? A hundred and fifty, isn't it? Oh no, it can't possibly be three hundred. Don't you remember I'd given you Rs. 150 last month, a hundred-rupee note and five tenners?"

Supratim had gone bonkers trying to calculate his wife's losses. She was no match for Supratim, the smart businessman and sharp area sales manager, and had put him to shame. Poor Aditi had no option but selling off the saris at a loss and keeping the rest for herself. That was the end of her business venture. So many people in this same building complex owed her money, amounting to nearly three or four thousand. There was no hope of ever retrieving the amount!

Aditi finished her dinner in glum silence. At night when she was braiding her hair before going to bed she said to Supratim,

"Did you really have to taunt me about your lost money before the boys?"

Supratim was absorbed in the newspaper. But he was looking at the share market rates and not the news. He found it impossible to go to sleep unless he caught up with the latest on stock exchange throughout the country. It was his obsession to keep track of the rise and fall of the various shares every single day. It was something like an addiction. He did not hear Aditi.

"What did you gain by ridiculing me before the boys?" repeated Aditi.

"What's wrong? What are you muttering about?" asked Supratim.

"You accused me of lying in their presence." There were tears in her eyes.

"Good heavens! I never called you a liar."

"Of course you did. Ask yourself honestly, didn't I tell you about my writing? Hadn't you said yourself that you'd fetch those magazines sometime and read them?"

"Oh, so that's why you're so peeved!" Supratim burst out laughing. It was so easy to tease her!

"I didn't call you a liar. I merely said that I didn't quite believe that you actually wrote anything special."

"Well, you never said so."

"Said what?"

"That you didn't believe me."

Supratim smiled. "Can anyone possibly say it to a bride? If you had told me then that you were a champion rider or an ace climber, even then I wouldn't have contradicted you."

"What dishonesty!"

"Not dishonesty, mere self defence. Who wants to look at a grumpy bride?"

Aditi did not reply but went on combing her long hair silently. She still needed quite some time to put it in order. Holding one end of the ribbon with her teeth, she wrapped the other end round her hair like a pony tail. That's how she was used to doing it up at night. It made her uncomfortable to leave it loose on the pillow. By the time she finished braiding her temper was cooled. Her anger, resentment and ire were like autumn clouds. Brief and short lived. Rain and sunlight went almost hand in hand.

She pulled out the loose strands of hair from the comb and blew them out of the window. "I felt so sorry to see Hemen Mama this morning."

"Why? Does he look particularly tragic these days?"

Aditi burst out laughing. Supratim loved to tease her, even now, despite the fact that he was almost verging on fifty.

"I meant, he looks totally transformed now. I remember the day he first came to our place with my uncle. I was totally bowled over by him. He must have been in his late thirties then and I was a student of first year, college. He looked so fantastic! Tall, slim, and fair with sharp Greek features. He wore thick glasses. He was just like you'd imagine a writer to look. He looks so thin and old now."

"Do you feel sorry?"

"Of course I do. He was so handsome once upon a time."

Supratim was marking the paper with a pencil. He took off his reading glasses and gave her a keen look.

"Sounds like you were in love with him."

"Wish I were" said Aditi with a mock sigh, "At least he'd have settled down then."

"What do you mean? Didn't he marry?"

"No. He was crazy about literature. It was his whole life. Edited some magazine, not a particularly popular one. Then he took up a job with a school in Alipur Duar."

"A broken heart? Why distant Alipur Duar of all places?"

"Could be. That's what we all thought."

"Who was the girl? Not you, I hope?"

"Don't be silly. He was so much older than I was, besides being my uncle's friend. He was almost like an uncle."

"In South India uncles and nieces share a romantic relationship" said Supratim yawning, "It's quite possible that he was a silent lover of yours. Otherwise what prompted him to seek you out after all these years?"

"It's not like that at all. I told you he used to admire my writing."

Aditi came to the bed and sat down. "Hemen Mama has started another magazine after returning to Calcutta. He asked me to write something for it."

"That's good. Write by all means. But what will you write, a story or a poem?"

"I don't think it's that easy to start writing again at my age."

"Why not? Write what you can. He is going to publish it in any case, isn't he?"

Supratim lit a cigarette and puffed leisurely. "You keep saying that you don't know what to do with your time. Spend it this way. Or are you too lazy to try?"

The accusation hurt Aditi to the quick. How could he call her lazy? Didn't he know how she had spent her time from the day they were married? Looking after her father and mother-in-law, cooking for her brothers and sisters-in-law when they were busy attending college and the university, running after two young and unruly sons? How much leisure did Aditi have then? Gradually, years later, Supratim rose to a better post. Her brother-in-law found a good job and shifted to Lucknow. Her two sisters-in-law were married. Her father and mother-in-law passed away within a year of each other. Then they bought this new flat in Salimpur and moved in here. But even after that, how much leisure did Aditi have?

Supratim had never had to bother about the house or his family or the education of the boys. He only handed her the money for running their life. For Supratim, his office was his whole world. His ultimate pilgrimage. The only difference lay in his destinations. In those days he used to visit Maldah, Siliguri, Murshidabad and Jalpaiguri. Now he flew to places like Bhubaneshwar, Ranchi, Patna, Guwahati and Cuttack.

In the midst of all this her sons had cleared their Secondary and Higher Secondary examinations. Not just anyhow but with flying colours. Had it happened without her active involvement in everything? It was she who had rushed to their schools every now and then, found tutors and tutorial classes, kept track of who was faring badly in a subject and did something about it. It was she who had organized everything – Papai's cricket practise in the morning, Tatai's swimming practise in the evening, their constant needs and requirements. Had she looked after all this with laziness? She had both boys virtually breathing down her neck, never having a moment to herself. And it was not just her boys. She had to shop for the entire year choosing each and every item carefully. Shopping that included buying cleansers for the toilet as well as selecting matching ties for Supratim. It was Aditi who had done everything single handed.

And yet Supratim, who knew it all, accused her of being lazy!

Yes, now she had plenty of time on her hands. The long afternoons. Languid evenings that melted into dusk. Her boys no longer clung to her as they once did. They even had a cook to look after all the meals since her surgery for appendicitis some time back. Papai now did some of her shopping for her. And Supratim never returned home before nine. She now had all the time in the world in her empty flat.

Yes, she had time. But a lot of precious time had been lost as well.

It was but natural. Time and tide waited for none. Could one bathe in the same tide a second time? Was there any point trying to take up writing once again and making a laughing stock of herself? Perhaps it was wiser to put up with the accusation of laziness.

Aditi stood up with a small sigh. She often felt thirsty at night. She decided to keep some water in the room.

Supratim put out his fag. "Listen, get me my file from the table," he said to Aditi.

"Are you going to work now? Won't you come to bed?"

"Just a few minutes. I won't be long."

Aditi handed him the file and came to the kitchen. The milk on the gas was cold now and ready for the fridge. There had been a lot of burglaries of late. A thief had climbed up the rainwater pipe only the day before yesterday. Burglars were like gypsies. They never stayed in the same place for long. But even then there was no harm being a little extra careful. She shut the kitchen windows and secured them carefully with a piece of string. They had moved in here nearly ten years ago but the flat had not been whitewashed for the last four years.

The kitchen walls looked grimy. They simply must get the whitewashing done this winter. Perhaps she should get some more tiles put in the kitchen as well. It would be quite the thing.

Aditi came out of the bathroom, picked up a jug of water and peeped inside her sons' room as a matter of course. The big light was switched off. Tatai was asleep in his bed. He always went to bed early after a hot argument and fell asleep instead of watching television. He was still a child at heart. Papai was studying in the light of the table lamp. He never touched books during the day. Night was his chosen time for study. Keeping awake was never a problem. He just needed one thing to keep awake. Coffee. He had acquired the addiction right from his Higher Secondary days. But Aditi didn't give him strong coffee even now. She made about three cups of milky coffee and kept it in the flask for him. Coffee addiction wasn't all that bad. Thank God he hadn't taken to smoking like Tatai. Tatai, despite his tender years reeked of tobacco. But when she had told Supratim he merely laughed and said, "Well, I started smoking at his age too. Like father, like son!"

Aditi returned to her own room. Keeping the water jug on her dressing table she lowered the speed of the fan. It got quite chilly in the early mornings. The fan made it worse. Both windows of her bedroom faced the north so it was colder than the other rooms. In winter it felt frosty even during the day.

Supratim had put down the mosquito net and was reading

the file in bed. Aditi peeped inside. "You have forgotten the coverlets even today."

"Sorry. It quite escaped my mind."

"How can you be so forgetful? You have to do just two things in the house. Putting down the mosquito net and keeping the pillows and coverlets in place. I don't see how you can manage to forget even that."

"I said I'm sorry, didn't I? Just pick it up yourself."

Supratim shoved his glasses and the file behind his pillow. "I don't need the coverlet. It's you who feel shivery even when it isn't cold"

"Indeed! Who keeps coughing early in the morning? Not me!"

She pulled out the coverlets and put them inside.

Someone in a nearby flat was watching a film on cable television. The sound of people shouting floated into the room. There was the clutter of falling utensils in another flat. There was a sudden scream from yet another. The last train to Sealdah was blowing its loud whistle. All noises seemed strangely alive during this hour.

Aditi got into bed and switched off the light.

Supratim was lying on his back. "I've a piece of good news. I had forgotten to tell you before."

"What is it?"

"No shared taxis for me from the next month. The office

will provide me with a car."

"Really?"

"Yes. But it won't be exclusively mine. Sen of the accounts department lives in Jadavpur. He'll also travel with me. But in office the car will be entirely under my control."

"I see."

"Don't sound so tepid. Do you realise what it means? It means I'm getting more important. As far as I know, our head office in Mumbai is now taking an active interest in Supratim Mazumdar. I'm likely to get a big salary hike as well."

"Sounds good."

"Good but it has its own problems. I hear Jameson India is going to join up with our company. It's hardly going to be a proper amalgamation. Theirs is such a huge company, they're quite likely to swallow us. Not that it will matter so far as salary and perks are concerned. But it will mean a whole lot of strangers over my head. I've been working in this company for nearly 25 years now. I don't know how I'll stand being bossed by a pack of strangers. I have a working pattern of my own. Supposing they don't see eye to eye with me?"

Aditi listened to his words carefully. She knew that her husband was a sincere worker who had made his way up because of sheer hard work. He was a dedicated worker and really loved his company. He was honest, forthright, and scrupulous and looked down on taking bribes. Wasn't it natural that she should be interested in hearing about his work? She got to see a bigger, unknown world through his eyes which was a real gain. His words brought on a dream of happy slumber for Aditi. They sounded like a lullaby to her ears. Supratim spoke on alone. Being a salesman he was used to doing all the talking. It hardly mattered to him whether anyone listened to him or not. Words were his bread and butter. Words spelt happiness for him. Words also brought on sleep.

Aditi was fast asleep. But she woke up all of a sudden. The bird in the balcony was fluttering its wings loudly. She shook Supratim awake. "There must be a cat in the balcony. Do go and see."

Supratim was asleep too. He was annoyed at being rudely awakened. "Let it flutter away. No cat can come in though the grill."

Aditi put on the light. "The poor bird sounds really scared. Do go and drive the cat away."

"You do it. It's your bird. Don't bother me."

"Please go. I don't feel like getting up."

"You're the absolute limit!" Supratim got up and stamped out to the balcony. He returned almost immediately. The bird was silent now.

"It was a cat, wasn't it?"

"Yes, sitting on the wall far away. Your bird's a bloody coward."

"Is it still on the wall? Then it will start fluttering again."

"No, it won't. I've covered the cage with a sheet. The bird won't see a thing now."

Supratim put out the light.

Chapter Three

A pebble thrown in a silent pool brings on ripples. But how long do the ripples last? A bare ten or twenty seconds, or at best, a minute. Such ripples are gentle and powerless. The outward edge of the weak and placid circle does, perhaps, touch the side of the pool somehow but it is difficult to feel its presence. Looking at the pool one can hardly guess that a pebble had fallen into it just a short while ago.

Hemen Mama's sudden visit was something of this nature. It had caused a mild ripple in her pool of memories, reminding her of a happy time. She could feel that ripple of joy for a short while. But it soon subsided into a tranquil quiet. The wave broke against the shore of her everyday existence, unable to bring about any change.

Aditi felt secure, spending her time with the caged bird, thinking of her husband and her children, moving along with time with tiny steps.

Or perhaps she wasn't really spending her time.

How did it matter either way? Time was not meant to stand still, it would move on whatever happened. And it was moving on. Supratim went on a tour to Guwahati last week and spent three days there. Tatai spent the weekend at Digha with his friends. Papai was burning the midnight oil as earnestly as ever. Weren't these part of her own 'spent' time ?

Aditi stood before the open cupboard trying to select a sari. The hangers held them in a neat row. There were many, all really expensive. Kanjeevaram, Dhakai, Kalakshetram, Baluchari, Bomkai, and Chanderi – she had them all. Supratim made it a point to select and buy her saris during the pujas, right from the time they were married. Most of them were in bright colours. Supratim felt that he wasn't getting his money's worth unless he went for really flashy colours.

Aditi pulled out the dark orange Kanjeevaram. No, this wouldn't do as it was slightly dirty. She had worn it at a relative's wedding last summer and had forgotten to get it washed soon after. She hardly found sufficient occasions to wear all these saris. But Supratim went on buying them and they hung in her cupboard adding on to the row. Aditi picked out a Bomkai silk. It was a bright peacock blue. She didn't really enjoy wearing such flashy colours any more. But there was no help for it. She was bound by an unspoken contract to Supratim according to which she had to wear saris of his choice when visiting his friends although she was free to wear what she liked at other places. Well, she may as well wear the blue one, then. At least this one was less bright than the others.

As she ironed the matching blouse she heard Tatai's voice ordering the cook. "Sabitadi, give me something to eat, quick. I have to go out right away."

Aditi peeped out of the door. "You have barely come in. Where do you want to go at this time of the evening?"

"I have work, Mom."

"What sort of work?"

"A special sort"

Tatai ambled inside his own room. Aditi followed. "What on earth is the matter with you? I don't ever see you reading a book these days."

Tatai lay in bed with his head on his palms. "Who told you I don't study? I always study at the crack of dawn."

"Don't talk rubbish. You never wake up before seven in the morning."

"Well, after seven, then."

"That's a lie. Do you think I don't know what you do? You pore over the newspaper for hours, slip out for a while, and then dash off to college. Where does studying come in ?"

Tatai closed his eyes and didn't reply.

That was Tatai all over. Bone lazy about studies. He never sat down to it without being forced. Aditi had smacked him for his ways so many times. He'd bunk classes and go off to see films. Play hooky during tutorials. Miss classes whenever he could. And strangely enough, he never fared badly in his exams.

Supratim returned home exactly at half past seven. He immediately started off his usual hullabaloo, the kind that inevitably preceded his going to a party.

"What's this? Why have you taken out my cream kurta? I don't want it. Get the tasar set out. Let me see how you look. You should have worn a bigger dot on your forehead. I suppose my electric shaver is in Papai's room. Why don't you find it instead of sitting still? Oh, you don't have any sense at all. Do you really expect me to wear this jacket with that kurta? And why don't you wear a little more lipstick? Your face looks dull. You never even told me how you like the bouquet! Got it made specially from the New Market. Paid Rs. 230 for it. The wretched fellow was asking for three hundred...." and so on

Aditi felt a trifle uneasy at the time of going out. Papai had not returned as yet. Sabita had finished cooking dinner and had left already. Surely they could have waited for another five or ten minutes. Supratim never came home early when they had to go out in the evening. And once he was home he refused to wait even for a minute. So Aditi was compelled to leave the keys of her flat with her neighbour and leave with him.

Rupak's house was at the other end of the city, way beyond the Behala crossing. It took around twenty minutes to reach there in a taxi. This evening it was likely to take even longer as there was a biggish traffic jam near Mahabirtala.

The night was moving on. There was a distinct nip in the air. A chilly breeze with a tinge of biting cold blew about them. And yet it was only autumn now. The winter was sure to be a severe one this year.

Aditi put up the window glass and covered her neck. Supratim leaned back on the seat humming a tune.

"You could have worn something warmer instead of that fancy jacket" said Aditi.

"Don't fuss. It isn't that cold yet. Guwahati was really chilly. In any case I'll be totally warmed up by the time I return."

Aditi turned her face away. Tatai had left the house wearing just a flimsy T-shirt. She hoped he wouldn't catch a chill. He used to suffer from cold throughout the winter when he was young. But it improved when he took to swimming. But he had given up swimming after his Higher Secondary exams so the old trouble was back with a vengeance. God alone knew how many cigarettes he smoked each day!

"You are never bothered by what happens at home" Aditi remarked casually, " Have you noticed your younger son lately?"

Supratim placed the bouquet on the seat of the car and lit a cigarette. "Why, what's the matter with him?"

"Nothing much, except that he is perpetually putting on a 'don't-care' air these days"

"It's normal at his age. He's just growing wings. He's trying them out." Supratim threw the match stick out of the window.

Aditi grew thoughtful. She didn't usually discuss the boys with Supratim as she thought them to be a part of her personal domain. But she could not stop herself today.

"I don't like Tatai's friends."

He has always had all kinds, some good some bad. I think it's good to have some bad boys as friends. It helps maintain one's balance. Don't you know that one is often injected with comparatively harmless germs in order to keep the harmful ones at bay? It helps build up one's resistance."

Supratim shook his head with the air of one experienced. "Not all my friends were goody-goody ones. I had a very close friend called Sitesh who was once involved in a mass-rape case. But being friends with him didn't have any adverse effects on me."

"Perhaps not, but..."

"Don't coddle him, for goodness' sake! Let him grow up! How is he to know the difference between the good and the bad if he doesn't mix with both kinds? Besides, there's bound to be something good in the worst of boys. Sitesh was a wonderful speaker. He could convince anybody about something in two minutes flat. I always tried to pick up his technique of presenting a case. I learnt a great deal from him. At the end of the day what really matters is the good points one is able to pick up from the others."

Aditi felt depressed. Whenever she tried to discuss her sons Supratim inevitably took their side, seeing everything from their point of view.

"I didn't say his friends are bad. I merely said that I don't like them. They are a queer sort, uppity, upstart-ish. They have the typical airs of a business class. They own cars and mobikes, wear flashy clothes and ...."

"That's good. Your son is on his way to acquiring class and has made a pack of classy pals.."

"Classy indeed! He's fast turning into a spendthrift. He took fifty rupees from me just yesterday and wanted some more today.."

"Indeed?" Supratim threw his cigarette out of the window and smiled, "The fellow took a hundred from me yesterday."

"Why didn't you tell me before?" asked Aditi in a harsh tone.

"What's the use? He just wanted some, I suppose" Supratim raised his hand just the way Tatai did when he was embarrassed, "Very well, I shan't give him any more money."

Aditi made a face. He hated Supratim's way of pampering the boys. Something he had acquired from day one. The two brothers always fought when they slept in the same cot so Supratim promptly bought two separate ones for them. Tatai refused to touch Papai's hand-me-downs, even books, so she had to throw them away. The boys wanted two of every single thing. Table, chair, cupboard, bookshelves. The younger wanted identical things that the elder possessed. Aditi had once bought a big water bottle for Papai. Tatai's was slightly smaller in size.

Tatai wept the whole evening. Aditi had said, "Cry all you want to, but you will use the water bottle that I've got you." Within two days Supratim bought him another, identical to the one that Papai had. What a way of spoiling a kid! Papai never asked for things but Supratim gave him the very best. When going on their annual puja shopping spree Papai would keep looking at the most expensive suit and kept stroking it without actually asking for it. But Supratim would buy it for him instantly, no matter how much it cost. Aditi felt it to be wastage and it made her see red. What was the use of squandering six or seven hundred for something Papai would outgrow in a matter of days? But Supratim saw things differently. "For whom do I earn, Madam?" he would ask laughing, "Isn't it for the boys?" What could she say to that? Her opinion hardly mattered to him, despite the fact that she was his wife and the children's mother.

The taxi had covered most of the way. They were now at the Taratala crossing leaving New Alipore behind. There were not many people on the road, possibly on account of the sudden spurt of cold. There were a few cars but not too many.

Supratim touched Aditi's shoulder. "Why are you so determined to dampen your mood? After all we are going to participate in a celebration. Look here, don't you know that it's you who steer our lives? All of us are under your control. Just tell us what you like and don't like straight out and see if we go by it or not."

Aditi did not reply. She merely sighed, holding the air in her breast for a long time. Then she tried to switch on a smile. Did she succeed?

Rupak's house was a two-storeyed one. A brand new house, though it was quite small. But it was right on the main road. Rupak was upstairs when their taxi arrived and dashed down at once. "Why are you so late?"

"Couldn't help it" said Supratim pointing at Aditi, "Took simply ages wearing her make-up. And of course, choosing what to wear. I won't have this one, nor that one ...."

Aditi glared at Supratim and was about to contradict him when she saw him shaking Rupak by the hand, wishing him many happy returns of the day. " So you really managed to stay together for twenty-five long years, you lucky dog!"

Rupak took the bouquet from Aditi's outstretched hand and said in a voice tinged with pride, "Of course I did. And I hope to spend another twenty-five."

"That's the spirit!" said Supratim slapping him on the back, "What booze have you got?"

"Anything you'd care to name. Whiskey, rum, gin, vodka, brandy. I had champagne as well but it's exhausted now. You people turned up so late!"

"Never mind. Who else has arrived?"

"Everyone. Somen, Thathagata, Aniruddha. Only Deepak couldn't make it. The poor chap's in a real soup." Rupak, who had donned a dhoti and kurta for the occasion, turned to Aditi.

"Why don't you go in? Seema and the others are waiting for you."

The party was in full swing. After all, a silver wedding is a very special affair and Rupak had left no stones unturned to make it a success. Apart from his friends there were quite a few relatives. His brothers, sisters with their respective spouses and other in-laws. The hall upstairs was covered with flowers and silver paper. The amplifiers blared out dance music under a soft greenish light. The glass covered balcony had been turned into a bar. Rupak's two daughters were also serving drinks. Dance and booze flew simultaneously. People were swaying in rhythm, some out of rhythm, in a variety of clothes. Sari, salwar-kamiz, jeans, dhoti, kurta-pyjama. Everything was a dance costume tonight.

Aditi sat in a corner of the hall with Kasturi, Sudipa, Gopa and Pranati, the wives of Supratim's friends. Seema, Rupak's wife flitted across from one guest to another like a butterfly despite her weight. She had dressed up with great care tonight. A gorgeous white Banarasi sari, flowers in her hair, heavy jewellery. And yet Aditi could detect a shadow of weariness in her eyes. Was it due to today's exhaustion or was it the mark of aging?

No one has anything specific to say in parties like these. The same kind of comments and remarks go round in circles. Sometimes a chance comment brings on a shower of laughter. Sometimes words turn to mundane conversation. Both Kasturi,

Somen's wife, and Sudipa, Tathagata's wife, had classy jobs. The others usually listened to their comments carefully during such get-togethers. But their topics of conversation were always one and the same. Clothes, jewellery, and films. Gossip. Husband, children and home. Maids and in-laws. Even then everyone listened to them attentively. Perhaps because they expected something special from them. Most of them had glasses in their hands. Others made attempts at dancing because it was the done thing in such gatherings.

Aditi had also tried everything. But she always made sure to keep her drinking within limits. Not because of any moral inhibition but because alcohol tended to aggravate her headaches and acidity. But she rather liked such gatherings though she could not let her hair down as completely as the others. She enjoyed watching them even though she couldn't be as heady herself. That was her way.

Supratim, on the contrary, let himself go totally at parties. He gulped down his first peg and was totally sozzled by the time he had downed three or four more. He spoke loudly, danced wildly and broke into ear-splitting laughter without any rhyme or reason. Sometimes he even broke into song in his off-key voice and totally wrong words. Such things do happen in parties. People tended to egg Supratim on and watch the fun themselves.

But Aditi did not let it happen this time and forced Supratim to leave before it was eleven, saying they'd have trouble finding a taxi.

They were now on their way home in a taxi. Supratim rested his head against the seat of the car. "The party was rather a dim one tonight" he said.

"You shouldn't say so! You were singing "John Jaani Janardan rum-pum-pum-pum-pum" at the top of your voice" answered Aditi, "Why do you always break out like that the moment you're drunk?"

Supratim sat up straight. "You know very well that Supratim Mazumdar never gets drunk. I was merely letting my hair down. If I can't let go even at a friend's place, where else can I do it? Everyone needs to let off steam sometimes."

"Don't forget that you're getting old."

"Old? Age is merely a mental fixation. You are as old or as young as you feel."

A wild breeze blew outside. This time it was Supratim who put up the window glass. Then he lit a cigarette with shaky hands in his third or fourth attempt. "Had age really been a factor such a thing couldn't have happened to Deepak. They are trying for a legal separation at their age because Sharmila has fallen for a thirty-year-old boy."

Aditi laid her head against the seat. "But I heard a totally different story. It's Deepak who is running after an old woman."

Supratim burst out laughing. "Is that so? Let them go to hell. Come to the point. Don't forget, we're fast approaching our silver wedding ourselves."

"Oh no, not the silver wedding. It will be our 24th wedding anniversary this July."

"Very well, next year then" said Supratim yawning, "I'll have a far more gorgeous function at our silver wedding. We'll exchange garlands and have the shehnai players as well. They'll play from the morning as they do at weddings."

"For shame! How can you talk like this with grown up sons.?"

"They'll be the hosts" laughed Supratim. "They will be the ones to organize their parents' wedding. I had no control over my own wedding but my silver wedding is going to be just the way I want it."

"How you love to tease!" said Aditi.

"I'm not teasing. I'm dead serious about the whole thing." Supratim turned his face and gave Aditi a keen look. "The way we've spent twenty-five years of our life together, do you think it's nothing to write home about? One may get married several times but reaching a silver wedding is a milestone in one's life. Won't I demonstrate to the world all that I have achieved during the time?"

Aditi didn't laugh any more. The word "achievement" rang like a bell in her heart. What had she achieved in twenty-five years? A husband, children, a home, wealth, and security? Or getting lonelier and lonelier with the growing years? A broken, splintered solitude? Which?

Chapter Four

Alakesh lay in bed, his leg in plaster. He had hurt himself falling down from a running bus. Aditi went round to see him at their Amherst Street house after her niece called her up and told her about the accident.

Aditi rarely came to her parental house these days. The tie had been a far stronger one when her mother was alive and she would drop in at least once or twice a week if not every day. It was now more than four years since her mother had passed away. The bond grew weaker with every passing day. She only made it on special occasions now, such as bhai phota, bijoya oı some other family event. The same was true of her brother and his wife. They hardly ever came to look her up. It was Tultuli, her niece, who kept the bond alive, dropping by every now and then at her aunt's place on her way back from the university.

Aditi drew up a chair beside her brother's bed. "Well then, how on earth did you manage to fall from the bus?"

Alakesh, lying down with a glum face cheered up visibly at

the sight of his sister.

"Thought I'd manage to jump up the steps. But my feet let me down."

Aditi touched the plaster that covered her brother's right knee. "Is it a proper fracture or just a sprain?"

"A dislocated bone. It will set in time, I guess, but I'll have to remain in bed for six whole weeks."

"So, now you've done it to your right knee as well!"

"Do you remember about my left one?"

"Don't I just? The way you staggered back home from the field leaning on the shoulders of Rinka-da and Nera-da, moaning and groaning, was a sight to behold! Then you burst into tears and howled about how you couldn't play at all that season. Mother sat up the whole night applying a hot lime-and-turmeric plaster on your knee and father grumbled away about why you had to play at all if you couldn't manage better than this."

"Yes and when I returned from the hospital with my leg in plaster you stood by the door clapping your hands and screeching that stupid rhyme about where I'd been and got myself all bashed up!"

Everyone burst out laughing at the way Alakesh said it. His wife, daughter, son and Aditi herself. But there ran an undercurrent of pain beneath all this laughter. Aditi could feel it every time she came here. The old house had completely lost its original looks. Now seepage blinked out of its thick, damp walls on all sides. And yet, every time she stepped in here, her lost youth and childhood seemed to clasp her by the waist and tug at her sleeves without any apparent reason. Why did it happen? Was it because she was growing old? Was it because her mother was no longer there? Because she had been too involved running her own life all these years and never had the time or the inclination to look back? Or was it because of the partition of coolness that now stood between herself and her brother?

How little it took to change a relationship and make it go sour! Alakesh had made Aditi sign some papers soon after their mother's death. She had not even bothered to ask him what they were or check what she was signing on. It had been enough that her brother had asked her to do it. It was much later that she realised that he had made her sign away all rights to their parental house and made it appear as though she had done it of her own free will. She still remembered how Supratim had scolded her when he got to know about it.

"Whether you chose to accept your share of the property or not, shouldn't he have offered it to you at least? Or tell you what he was asking you to sign on? And hats off to you too, Aditi! You're not illiterate, dash it! How could you sign on a document without checking what it was?"

The incident had touched her on the raw. She knew that her brother's job was nothing to write home about. He had started as a mere lower division clerk and now headed the upper division ones. He did not have the same means as Aditi. His son was as yet unsettled. He still had to marry off his daughter. Could Aditi possibly have refused to give up her share in his favour? Certainly not! So where was the need to trick her into doing it the way he had done?

Alakesh had come to get another paper signed a few days later. It was the document of her mother's fixed deposit in the bank. Aditi did not spare him this time and had blurted outright "Do I have to give up my share of this as well?"

Her brother was stunned into silence at her words and finally stammered, "It's not a big amount. Just ten thousand rupees or so. Do you really want your share, Khuku?"

"The amount does not matter" Aditi had replied, pulling a long face, "Just think, if I'd been your brother instead of your sister, could you possibly have made me sign away everything keeping me cleverly in the dark?"

Alakesh had turned pale at her words and replied, "No need to make an issue of it. I'll give you your share."

His wife, seated beside him, blurted out "Why didn't you tell us point blank that you wanted your share of the property? You are so well off, we had taken it for granted that you wouldn't care one way or the other."

Aditi had not succeeded in convincing them that it was not the actual signing away that she minded but the way in which he had done it. It was wrong of him to assume that Aditi had no right to the property. Wrong to overlook the fact that it belonged to her equally. It was an insult to her right and it was wrong to go about it the way he had done. She had not even accepted her share of the money from him. But the bitterness had remained. She had not stepped into her ancestral home for a whole year, not until her mother's first death anniversary.

Time had played its inevitable role in lightening the resentment with the passing of days. But the breach had never healed completely. There remained a little gap somewhere along the way. Was it a natural thing for unseen termites to destroy the bond between siblings when the parents were no more and transform the old ties of childhood, the love, pranks and heartaches of the time into something meaningless? Or did some of it remain as scattered memories as seemed obvious from Alakesh's words? The 53-year-old brother went down memory lane with his 45-year-old sister, picking up pearls from the forgotten sands of time. Runtu and Tultuli made comments as their mother stood by, tea and sweets in her hand. A wonderfully happy picture of family life. But there was a hidden thorn somewhere.

Winter had already arrived and made its presence felt. Even this late noon felt downright chilly. The house, built on a rear plot, lacked both light and air. Chill dripped from its old walls. Aditi drew her shawl cosily around her as she sipped her tea and asked, "Any new marriage proposals for Tultuli?"

"Yes, there was one" answered her sister-in-law, "A junior officer in an insurance company. But your niece turned him down."

"Why? Wasn't he good looking?"

"I've no idea why. Better ask her yourself. I don't think it is right for girls to be so fearfully choosey."

"Well, he was awfully short and as dark as a tarred road, Pishi" said Tultuli making a face.

"Well, you are no beauty, either" said her mother in an angry voice, "I tell you, it was a good match and the boy's people really liked her."

"I don't see how that matters" cried Tultuli, "I have a mind of my own. Shouldn't I have a say in what concerns me? I've told you to stop looking around. Let me find a job first"

"Which means you don't want your parents to find a suitable boy but prefer to find one yourself?"

"Why not?" said Aditi laughing, "At least she won't be able to blame you afterwards!"

Then she looked at Tultuli and asked, "Do you have someone in mind?"

Runtu had been listening to them silently all this time. Now he said, "Your Jadavpur University is an absolute Vrindaban where people pair off all the time. It would be surprising if she didn't."

Aditi bit her lips in amusement. "Is it Vrindaban or do you

mean Nabadwip, the land of instant marriages? Tatai says the boys and girls at Jadavpur pair up the moment their eyes meet! Is that true, Tultuli?"

"Has Tatai really said that? Asked Tultuli pretending to be annoyed, "I'll box his ears the next time I see him."

Alakesh smiled though the discussion made him feel somewhat uncomfortable. He sat up in bed placing his plastered foot carefully.

"Tell me, Khuku, how is Papai getting on with his preparations?"

"Not too bad, he says."

"That's what he always says and then goes on to do brilliantly" added Runtu.

"Has he decided yet what he's gong to do after he graduates?" asked Alakesh.

"Do his Masters and then go for research. I guess he means to stick to academics."

"Why don't you ask him to take the civil service exams? It would be wonderful to have an IAS or an IPS officer as one's nephew."

Aditi herself thought along the same lines. How nice to have a district magistrate for a son who had a large bungalow to flaunt and go around visiting him, going about in his jeep ....

But one never could predict the future or know for certain what was going to happen.

"Papai is far too shy to make a strict administrator. It's Tatai's cup of tea, in fact" remarked Runtu.

Shibani, Aditi's sister-in-law, sighed audibly. "You are so lucky, Aditi. Both your sons are absolute gems. I wonder what my poor Runtu is going to do."

Runtu looked uncomfortable at his mother's words and Tultuli said, "Stop it, ma. Are you suggesting that he's a good-for-nothing?"

Aditi looked at her brother, the one-time football player who had reigned supreme in the fields with lightning in his steps, sitting as still and expressionless as a zombie, an unseeing look in his eyes. Was he worried about his son's future too?

Aditi had hoped her brother would ask Supratim to find a job for his son. It was four long years since Runtu had graduated. Not that he had been sitting idle all this time. He had been coaching a lot of youngsters from primary school. He had also done some computer course. But he had always been an indifferent student. But even then Supratim would have managed to find him a job had her brother requested him. They often hired young boys as salesmen. Besides, he had many contacts in different fields. Agents, distributors, clients. And Aditi could have pressurized him if he took too long over it.

But her brother had refused to say anything and she knew that he wouldn't. Ever.

Was it because of the old resentment that continued to linger despite everything? Or was it because he didn't care to lower himself in her eyes more than he had already done? Or did he expect Aditi to do it without being asked? And Runtu hardly ever visited his aunt. Was it because of some sort of inferiority complex?

After a few more inane exchanges of words Aditi stood up to leave, taking a few deep breaths unconsciously. The musty smell was far from pleasing but Aditi drew it in eagerly as she discovered the yellow tints of childhood, the crimson tint of her growing up years and the blue tint of her lost youth mixed up in the mustiness. Did she feel them because she no longer had any right to the place?

As she walked down the road she decided to take the train from Sealdah instead of going by bus. She stopped by a fruit shop on her way, picking up grapes for Supratim, oranges for Papai and pears for Tatai. By the time she pushed her way out to the Dhakuria station through a steady stream of office crowd darkness had already settled all around. As she stepped into the house she started in surprise. Hemen Mama was here again, seated on her sofa, chatting away with Papai. He wore the same clothes that he had done the last time except that he now wore a white shawl instead of a cotton wrap. Spreading out his hands in welcome like the master of the house he said, "Welcome home, Aditi."

All at once her hidden blues seemed to take to their wings bringing on a genuinely happy smile to her face, as she said, "When did you arrive?"

"Should I go by my watch or by what I feel?"

"What do you mean?"

"It's perfectly simple. Going by the watch, the time is 50 minutes. But I feel it's just a few minutes because I hardly noticed the passage of time talking to your son."

Aditi looked at Papai. "Did you offer grand-uncle some tea?"

"Of course he did and not just plain tea either. There were pastries and chips to go with it. He's been a perfect host."

Sabita was already there to cook supper. Aditi placed the fruits in the big glass fruit bowl on the table and asked, "Isn't Tatai back as yet?"

"Not yet" said Papai standing up. "I must look up Shaunak, now that you're back home."

Hemen interrupted, "But we haven't decided as yet whether there's any real conflict between science and literature. Shouldn't we settle the question before you leave?"

"Some other time. I really must go now." There was the glimmer of a smile as Papai made for his own room, slipped on his pullover and strode out.

Aditi shut the door behind him and complained, "You had promised to come soon the last time. Couldn't you have made it earlier? It's a whole month since you were here."

"Well, I haven't been exactly idle" said Hemen pulling out a magazine from his plastic bag, "Here, take a look. It's the latest issue. I've been really busy getting it launched."

Aditi turned over the pages carefully. It was quite a thick magazine comprising nearly a hundred pages of poems, stories, articles and other write-ups. Many of the poets were well known. It was a well produced, well turned out effort with an attractive cover that bore no illustration but just the name of the magazine in letters that resembled moving waves and the name of the editor in bright blue letters. Hemendra Narayan Mullick.

"Did you have this paper in mind when you asked me to write?"

"Don't call it a paper, it's a magazine" said Hemen giving Aditi an amused look.

"Yes of course. That's what I meant." Aditi smiled to cover up her confusion. "Did you launch it completely on your own?"

Hemen laughed outright. "Well, how could I expect a partner in work when life itself failed to provide me with one? But yes, I did have a couple of young boys to assist me when I was at Alipur Duar. They were my students."

Aditi had not taken his words seriously before but she now looked up, wonder in her eyes. "It must be pretty expensive to carry out such a project single handed."

"I got some money when I retired. I had no intention of hoarding it up uselessly. Besides, I have some friends who found me advertisements as well as some government ads. Once my registration comes through I don't really expect any problems."

Aditi did not understand all he said.

"You did the right thing, I guess" she said, "One must have something to do after one retires. Would you like another cup of tea?"

"I don't mind. Tea is always welcome when it's cold. Of course it's nothing compared to the freezing winters we had at the Duars. It was cold enough to make the tigers shiver."

Aditi called out to Sabita, asking her to make some more tea. Hemen Mama chatted away about winters in the hills and how a tiger had once barged into a cottage and pulled the rug off the landlord's back. He made it sound so hilarious that Aditi couldn't help laughing herself silly. She was amazed to find the once serious Hemen Mama so spontaneous and so much at ease. Indeed he had changed beyond recognition. He had been such a reserved young man when he had visited their house at Amherst Street in the past. Even when he smiled it used to be a quiet, measured one before.

He looked up all of a sudden and said, "Now give me what I've come to collect."

Aditi looked startled. "What do you mean?"

"Your story, of course". Go and get it and I'll go through it right now."

Aditi looked thunderstruck. "Story? Me?"

Hemen looked equally surprised. "Hadn't I asked you to write a story for my magazine when I came last?"

Aditi looked embarrassed. "Yes, you did .... But ...."

"But what?"

"I don't think I can write now. It's so long since I did."

The look on Hemen's face changed in a moment. "You had told me the same thing the last time," he said, suddenly looking serious, "And I had asked you to try. I was quite confident that you would succeed. Have you really made an effort?"

"Not quite, but ...."

"Why not? Didn't you find the time?"

Aditi couldn't bring herself to lie blatantly. "No, it's not that either. But I somehow couldn't quite try."

Hemen said no more and sat very still. He took off his glasses and polished them carefully for a long time and then said, almost to himself, "Not everyone has the talent, Aditi. But there is something each one of us can do. Some talent that he or she alone can hone to the best of his or her ability. It's a sin to do otherwise. A kind of moral suicide. I felt sure you had the required talent."

Aditi looked uncomfortable. But she enjoyed hearing his words.

"Perhaps I did .... once upon a time" she said softly, "But a lot of water has flown under the bridge since then, for the last 23 years. Bringing up my boys. Running my home ... A woman is often compelled to forget a great deal, Hemen Mama. Being single, you might not understand just what I'm talking about."

"That's just an excuse and a lame one at that. Women always try to find excuses for all that they leave undone. There are many things one can do despite running a home."

Hemen sounded really earnest as he said, "I remember reading a story of yours that I haven't forgotten to this day. I think it was published in one of your college magazines. It was about a girl who woke up each morning and stood staring at the mist, layers and layers of it. The deeper she walked into it the more she discovered – Rivers, forests, hills and waterfalls. But as soon as the mist lifted she found that there was nothing left. Nothing at all. Do you remember the story?"

A tiny pebble buried deep within a lake of consciousness seemed to lift up its head as Aditi nodded gently and replied, "Yes, I do. I had called the story, "Mists".

"Having once written a story like that can you honestly say that you can't write any more? Don't you have any buried thoughts in your heart that you'd like to give expression to? There's pen and paper right within your grasp. Try it and see. Now you have all the time in the world. Your boys are grown up and you are not staggering down under housework either."

Aditi couldn't but laugh at his words.

"I guess you have a point. But don't forget my advanced years. Mid-forties is hardly the age for creativity."

"You can't say that until you try. I admit that age does make some difference, laying a thin veil upon the imagination. But the veil's got to be lifted since you already possess the talent."

Sabita brought in the tea and looked curiously at the excited old man. Turning to Aditi she asked, "May I leave now? My cooking is done."

"Very well. How many rotis have you made?"

"About eighteen or so."

"Why on earth did you make so many? Didn't I tell you this morning that your Dada will dine outside?"

Sabita bit her tongue, looking embarrassed.

"Well, it can't be helped now. Hope you've shut the casserole tightly. The boys are going to be livid if the rotis get cold."

"I've shut it properly."

"OK, then. Come a little early tomorrow morning and don't forget."

Looking at Hemen Aditi added, "Do you now realise how many things I have to keep in mind?"

Hemen looked his usual placid self. "Do you know what Ramakrishna Dev once said? If you keep waiting for the waves to stop coming you can't possibly bathe in the sea," he said with a smile. A cool breeze swept across the room though the doors and windows were all shut. How did it manage to stray inside?

Hemen sipped the tea as he said almost to himself, "Do you know, Aditi, I never thought about you all these years, not even after I returned from Alipur Duar. Then I came across your uncle Bimal at Dalhousie Square one day. Perhaps he had gone there to draw his pension or something. I went to look him up at his Bhawanipore house some days later. As we sat talking he mentioned you out of the blue, so to speak. He spoke of how I had been to your place one evening with him and you had shown me your story. He told me that you were now happily settled with a successful husband and talented young sons and that you were totally involved in running your home. That's when I decided to visit you and remind you about your talent for writing. You did write well, had a clear insight into things and had the rare ability to choose just the right words. Why don't you try, really try once again? I'll come back after a month and expect a story from you when I do. May I?"

Aditi wasn't sure whether she had said yes or not. Probably she did. Or why else would Hemen smile at her before leaving? Aditi stood on the balcony for what seemed ages. The earth was growing colder. A thin mist crept along the open space. The street lights outside the gate looked dim and smoky. The concrete structures with their gaping doors and windows wore a spooky look.

There was no trace of Papai or Tatai. And no knowing when Supratim would be back. Aditi moved away from the grills and stood before the parrot touching the chilled cage. It felt icy cold. The bird was asleep. It dozed off the moment it grew dark outside but woke up the moment somebody stood before the cage.

"Well, parrot, do you want to write a story?" whispered Aditi. The parrot tried to look at her face in the darkness.

"What do you want to write about?" she whispered again, "Can you think of anything?"

The parrot moved.

"You doze all day long like an opium-eater and squeal every now and then. Can't you do anything more?"

The parrot stood silent.

"Why don't you try and write something just to please the crazy old man?"

The parrot moved again and shook its shoulder from side to side.

"Why don't you try writing your own story? About how your brother has broken his leg. Oh well, not quite broken but dislocated his leg. Try to remember how you loved him once and all the memories that centre around him and how it feels to see him now. After a long, long time. Forget the signing episode. Just focus on the brother and sister and how they now feel. Make up new incidents but keep the central theme running around the story, the gradual breaking up of a beautiful relationship."

Aditi looked at the cage intently. "What do you think? Do you feel you could really manage to do it?"

Chapter Five

Winter came to a grinding halt before the month of February was through. The sky remained overcast and it rained every now and then, not in wild torrents but in gentle drizzle. From where had this untimely army of clouds landed up? The net result was a sudden hike in the price of vegetables, especially cauliflowers. The sellers already threatened a further rise in price. People tended to fall sick left, right and centre. The merest drenching in the rain led to an epidemic of colds, coughs and fever.

Tatai was down with a sore throat and swelling of glands since yesterday. He had a dinner of milk and bread and obediently wrapped a muffler round his neck without having to be told. He sat before the TV wrapped up in Aditi's shawl watching the live telecast of the semi-finals of some tennis tournament between Andre Agassi and Michael Chang. The rally was beginning to hot up. Tatai thumped his fist on the table. "Come on, Agassi, do him in!"

Papai strolled in wearing a thick khadi kurta over his jeans and sat next to his brother.

"What's the score?" he asked fixing his eyes on the screen.

Tatai's eyeballs moved with the tennis ball. "Just what you'd expect. Agassi is leading, of course."

"He won't make it," said Tatai, his feet on the centre table.

"What makes you say that?"

"Tough for a playboy to make it in a game of tennis. One needs a great deal of concentration."

"Are you aware of his ranking? Chang's is nowhere near him"

"Ranking's not the last word in a game. Chang has far more go – probably because of his Chinese origin."

Tatai looked him full in the face. "Do you really think Agassi won't make it this time?"

"I do. Chang has more stamina and speed."

Before Tatai could finish his words Chang smashed down his racquet. The spectators cheered madly as the announcer blared, 'game to Chang'.

Tatai turned away with a glum face.

"Here they go again!" said Papai in a smooth voice, "Look carefully".

"Are you trying to bait me?" asked Tatai giving his brother a keen look.

"No, merely stating facts."

Tatai looked at him again and burst out laughing. "I'm determined not to shout tonight. It hurts my throat too much."

Supratim laughed too. He had been brushing his teeth and looking at the boys on the mirror in front of him. Brushing his teeth at night was a habit of long standing without which he felt dirty and uncomfortable. He gurgled several times and probed his gum with his tongue. He called out to Aditi who was in the kitchen arranging the piled up dishes in the sink.

"What is it?"

"Come here a moment, will you?"

"What's up?" she asked wiping her hands.

"Give me a matchstick. There's a fishbone lodged in my teeth."

"Take one of your own"

"Mine are the waxy kind, no good for probing."

Aditi fetched a couple from the kitchen and handed them with a wry face. Supratim stood probing and poking his gum.

"Got it out yet?" asked Aditi looking anxious.

"Not yet but I'll manage," Supratim said, probing deeper. "Are you through with your chores? I thought there was something you wanted to read out to us."

Aditi's heart missed a beat as she took a long breath to hide her excitement. But she managed to reply naturally. "Yes, I did. But let me get my kitchen organised first."

"Do hurry up. I want to turn in early tonight as I have to leave by 7.30 tomorrow morning."

"Shan't be a moment. Watch the TV until then."

Once inside the kitchen Aditi stood still, her heart thudding away like a piston. Something like what she used to feel in school just before the announcement of the results. She also felt a strange bout of shyness. Was she turning into a pig-tailed schoolgirl once again? Could she really bear to read out her story? What if they laughed?

She had settled down with pen and paper the day after Hemen Mama's visit. It was a quiet afternoon. How very tough the beginning had been! She had managed to think out a theme but just didn't know where to begin. No matter how she started it seemed quite wrong. She wrote a line, struck it out and wrote again. And then crossed it out all over again. When she managed to get two lines written the third eluded her completely. In vain she hunted for the right words going from one room to another – the bedroom, the drawing room, the dining space, the kitchen, the balcony, the bathroom, the works! But it seemed to be nowhere within her reach. She tore her hair in sheer exasperation. Tore up the paper. And got into a wild temper. But all to no purpose! The lazy afternoons that had once crawled by like a tortoise now rushed past like a whirlwind. But it was no good. Her maid stood staring at her curiously. "What on earth have you been up to, Boudi, scattering torn papers all over the place like a young child?" she asked disapprovingly.

Aditi had given up trying in despair. Her sister-in-law turned up the next morning with her two young daughters. They were in the midst of their Christmas holidays and had come to spend the day at their uncle's. They had made a real day of it, romping about all day long, turning the entire house upside down. By the time they left Aditi was at the end of her tether and took to her bed. She could not get up even the following day. After that it was holiday season for the entire family. Christmas, year-end, New Year's Day. Father and sons were determined to feast on delicacies – whether they remained at home or not – and demanded chocolate cakes, fruit cakes, biriyani, navratan pulao and what have you. Of course it was possible to get all these things from shops but no one cared to have them unless Aditi made them herself. Amidst all this baking and cooking Supratim took her out to the Diamond Harbour braving the mad rush of the New Year revellers. He really enjoyed it tremendously.

"Just look at the river and how it looks in the winter sun," he gushed, "Aren't the colours brilliant? Looks rather like our bath oil, doesn't it? If only we could produce things as steadily and constantly as the river does!"

But all these were a part of life. Aditi had finally managed to take them in her stride and make time for writing another quiet afternoon. She wrote, struck out, tore off the paper and wrote again, her pace slower than a snail's. After all, it was a creation and it is never easy to bring it about without just the right fusion of facts and the imagination. To create a character is like conceiving a baby, carrying it in one's womb and then giving it birth. Creating a set of characters meant the same. Putting one's heart, body and soul to work at one and the same time. All the more difficult if one was out of practise. It was really tough finding just the right word, the right expression. It was even tougher when, after writing a page or two, the story tended to run another way, contrary to one's thoughts. And one had to bring it back on track like a lost, wayward child and finally pin it down on paper. One day the sheer futility of her exercise drove Aditi to tears. She never imagined it would be so tough to give expression to her own story. What on earth had prompted her to promise Hemen Mama that she'd try?

By and by she got used to the idea and finally managed to write a story with what she felt to be the right descriptions and dialogues. But how was she to judge how good or bad it was? Aditi decided to swallow her feelings and ask her husband and sons to hear it.

Michael Chang had won the second set. The two players now faced each other in their third encounter. The flat soon rang with the announcement "Fifteen-Love". Aditi walked up to the sofa carrying her sheaf of papers, trying not to let the others guess how excited she felt. Looking at her husband and sons she cleared her throat and asked, "Shall I begin?"

"Well, you're not likely to let us off" said Supratim with an indulgent laugh, "Go ahead".

Aditi was about to start when Tatai said, "Just a moment,

Mom. Wait until the end of this game."

"Very well" said Aditi, counting the sheets. There were not too many, after all. Just ten sheets and a quarter.

Deuce! Both players were now abreast. Game for Agassi. Game for Chang. Advantage Agassi. Deuce. Advantage Chang. Deuce. So it went on and on. Never ending. Like Aditi's long silent afternoons. Supratim looked at Aditi's glum face and checked a smile.

"The game's going to take a long time yet," he said to his sons.

"Just a few more minutes, Dad."

"It's getting late, Tatai. I've to go to bed early tonight."

"Please Dad, just a little longer."

Game to Chang! The spectators cheered madly. Papai got up and switched off the TV.

"Come on, Mom. Read it."

Supratim leaned on the sofa and lit another cigarette. "So your Hemen Mama did succeed in making you write, eh?"

"The way he went on and on ...."

"He must be a jolly good pleader, quite out of the ordinary, if he could persuade you so easily. Even the poor salesgirls take hours to convince you about their products."

"I let them talk because I like spending time with them and not because I need convincing," said Aditi, her eyes on her story, "But of course Hemen Mama is a good talker. Ask Papai if you don't believe me."

"He's a big bore," said Papai.

"What do you mean?" asked Aditi amazed, "You had been chatting with him for hours, he told me."

"Listening to him, you mean! He rattled on and on about literature without letting me get a word in edgewise. As though there's nothing else worth talking about!"

"Indeed!" said Aditi thinking of the way Papai had looked that day. So polite and interested. Had he already become so adept at concealing his real feelings?

"If he talked of literature it's because it means so much to him" she added a little resentfully.

"Are you going to chatter all night?" asked Tatai impatiently, "Then I may as well watch the match."

"Hush Tatai" said Supratim, "Come on, Aditi, start."

Aditi had been feeling depressed at their reactions. But she cheered up at Supratim's words.

"Very well. The story is called "Cracks""

"Not an attractive title" said Supratim puffing away with his eyes closed, "You'd better change it."

"Listen to the story first. Then you'll see how the title fits."

"What did you say the title was? *Cracks*? Good heavens! Are you trying to be intellectual or something, Mom?"

"Well, no. It's a simple, homely story."

Aditi's story centred round a brother and sister. The brother, not too well off, had just had an accident and had hurt his head. The sister had come to see him after a gap of many long years. She was comfortably off. Her husband, a doctor, had a roaring practise. She suddenly remembered after reaching her brother's place that she was not carrying the customary fruits and sweets one always brought when paying a call. A formal custom. But hadn't their relationship now become a formal one too?

The telephone rang. Papai jumped up and snatched the receiver like a hawk. Covering the mouthpiece with his hands he said, "Just a minute, Mom."

Aditi looked up, smiled and put her story aside. There was a phone call for Papai every night just around this time for the last few days. It was a girl. When she picked up the phone the caller asked for Papai in an unsteady voice. If Supratim picked it up the line simply went dead. Was it a classmate? Strange for a classmate to sound so nervous. Papai always hung around the telephone around this time.

Tatai frowned and asked, "Are we going to wait for him?"

"Let him finish" said Aditi laughing.

"Then we'll have to wait forever"

"Don't be so impatient. Wait for a minute or two."

Tatai rubbed his hands impatiently and then stroked his aching throat.

"In that case I may as well find out what the score is," he

said, switching on the TV once again.

His eyes were glued to the screen. Papai was still whispering into the mouthpiece. So softly that they could barely see his lips move. A steady smile lurked about his lips.

Supratim nudged Aditi pointing to Papai's antics. Aditi told him not to stare in a hushed voice and added, "How do you like the story?"

"Too early to judge. Let me see how you tackle the theme."

"I meant the beginning."

"Not bad. Sounds like a family drama with brother and sister in the central roles. Hope you've kept some surprises."

"Listen to it first."

Supratim picked up the newspaper and studied the page on share markets. Not having his glasses at hand he held the paper close to his eyes. He took the pen from Aditi's hand and started marking the paper carefully, a frown on his face. Agassi had won the last set. Tatai's eyes gleamed as he made a face at his brother. Aditi tried her best to keep her enthusiasm alive.

"Well, Papai, are you through as yet?"

Papai raised his hand. "Just a minute, Mom."

Supratim put down his newspaper and yawned. "Better get on with it. I'm sleepy."

"Aren't we going to wait for Papai?"

"He can listen to it later or read it after it is published."

"Hemen Mama won't publish it unless it is good."

"Of course he will. Why else did he make you write it? There's no question of his not printing it. Come on, now. Hurry up. I've told you I've got to get up early tomorrow morning."

Tatai said, "Do I have to switch off the TV? Can't I just keep the sound off? Would that disturb your reading too?"

"Don't you want to listen to my story?" asked Aditi exasperated.

"Of course. But I'm listening with my ears. How does it matter if my eyes look at the silent screen at the same time? It just means both my organs are doing their respective work. You can ask me about your story later and check whether I've heard it or not."

Tatai switched off the sound, his eyes glued on to the screen once more. Papai continued to whisper into the mouthpiece. Aditi read on. Supratim made smoke rings overhead as he listened. Tatai's eyes were on the screen, steady and constant.

Aditi lost herself in her story. The story of a brother and sister, how close they were and how they grew apart, selfish interest bringing about the inevitable cracks in their relationship, until neither could recognise the other and were like two strangers. But even after a wall stood between them, did nothing remain? Was it all over for good? That was the question raised in her story. Aditi's voice grew hushed as she lost herself in the intensity of the emotions of her characters. She was no longer affected by the indifference of her listeners, the TV, the telephone or whether anyone was listening to her or not. She went on reading until the very end. Wiping her moist eyes she said in a semi-whisper, “Well, that’s it.”

Chapter Six

The parrot had been screeching away all afternoon, something it had taken to doing of late whenever Aditi sat down to write. Otherwise the bird had made positive strides in improvement. For one thing, it was not quite so wild. And though it had still not learnt to talk it could at least recognise the people of the house. When Supratim came by, it stood looking at him with a far away look in its eyes. When Papai or Tatai came near, it made a positive attempt to catch their attention by moving round and round in the cage, trying various tricks that resembled gymnastics, trapeze or back vault. But it was Aditi who mattered more than anyone else. It no longer screeched when she came to feed it like it used to do before but seemed to gaze at her with a fond look of understanding. Sometimes it took a few steps towards her, trying to come close. It was only in the afternoons that it grew so wild and unruly.

Summer had set in already. The rays of the sun got hotter by the hour. Standing on the open balcony in the afternoons felt like standing beside an oversize cauldron that heated up the entire atmosphere. The nor'easters hadn't arrived as yet or it might have cooled down the earth a little.

Aditi laid down her pen and came to the balcony. A blazing whirlwind covered the earth with a film of dust. Even the third floor balcony was full of grime. A piece of cellophane had blown in through the grill and was floating around aimlessly. Aditi grabbed it with her hand and came to the cage. Bending towards the parrot she asked gently, "Why are you screeching again? Do you feel hot?"

The bird shut its beaks the moment it saw Aditi and blinked at her silently.

"I know your tricks. You'd like me to stand before you all afternoon, isn't it?"

The parrot bent its head bashfully.

"No way, my love. I've work to do. I simply must complete my story. Hemen Mama wants it for his literary meet the day after tomorrow. If I don't have it ready he's going to bite my head off, not yours."

The parrot made some strange sounds.

"It's no use pleading" said Aditi, "I simply haven't the time to speak to you now."

The parrot screeched again.

"Shut up and no more noise" said Aditi, throwing away the piece of cellophane outside. She stood looking for a moment.

The cellophane did not fall on the ground. It floated away further and further. "Let it go where it will" said Aditi to herself as she returned to her room.

She lay down on her stomach on the floor; her pillow tucked under her breasts, and prepared to complete her story. She could neither write on the bed nor seated at a table. This was the only way she could really let herself go. The touch of the earth on her entire body as she lay on the floor seemed to give her added inspiration. She made quite a picture with her loose hair all over her face, the pallu of her sari on the floor and her feet up in the air as she scribbled away, her face reflecting a series of varied emotions. Sometimes she smiled, sometimes she frowned or muttered to herself, rolling on the floor. Sometimes she made faces. The emotions lurked about her visage like the varying colours of sunset. She returned to her story every now and then, reading it carefully. Had anyone made an attempt to capture her moods on a video camera undoubtedly he'd have thought her crazy. She often felt like one possessed during these creative afternoons.

"Cracks", Aditi's first story, had appeared in Hemen's magazine last month. All the uncertainty that had once made her so jittery had disappeared for good. Her first story had been a distinct hit. Hemen Mama's circle of critics was a fairly large one. He had insisted on their reading her story. Nearly all of them agreed that it didn't read like a first attempt. The language was mature, the treatment showed depth of understanding and what was most important, it led to a smooth climax. One of Hemen Mama's critic friends had actually come to her place with him to congratulate her in person. "It's ages since I read such a heart-warming story," he had told her, "Why haven't you been writing all these years? We shall expect many such stories from you in the future."

Aditi had felt a strange thrill of ecstasy at his words. She herself wondered why she hadn't taken to writing all this time. Was it because she had felt too content with her home and family to want anything more? Was she really too happy then? Was she any less happy now? Perhaps it was not quite that. She had taken all the small sorrows and disappointments in her stride, as an inevitable part of life. The heartbreaks and misunderstandings caused by her husband and sons constituted the very fabric of life without which it would seem flat, dull, and monotonous. It would be far truer to say that she had been happy. Or would it? Perhaps she had been neither happy nor unhappy, her life moving on as aimlessly as rolling water on the floor. She had no idea what direction it would take and didn't care. What really stood out now was the fact that she hadn't even been aware of this state of inertia. Perhaps she lacked that ability altogether. She had merely dug a well within her consciousness and lain there like an inanimate object all these years. Her writing had now lit up that well like a fresh ray of sunlight.

Or perhaps it was nothing so deep or philosophical. Perhaps

she had merely discovered a new toy to amuse herself with. Perhaps it was a temporary addiction, a momentary excitement. Something that had made waves in her heart for the time being. Would it subside as suddenly as it had come, pushing her back into her state of inertia once again? Aditi could not decide. There seemed to be no ready answer to her question. But it was a fact that she had really taken to writing this time. It had given her a new lease of life to discover that she had a special ability, quite apart from her ability to build up a home and bring up children. This new found realisation drew her like a magnet to her pen whenever the house was empty. There had been a time when she had hated being on her own. But now she craved it more than anything else and bitterly resented the many afternoons she had wasted in the past doing absolutely nothing. She was quite determined not to let it happen again. Why hadn't she guessed how thrilling it could be to pin down her thoughts on paper?

Aditi took up her pen eagerly. The doors and windows of the room were shut keeping out the rays of the hot summer sun. The tube light glowed softly. The fan twirled steadily overhead. Aditi wrote away furiously, tucking away the loose sheets under Supratim's pillow to stop them flying all over the place. She pulled the pillow away absent-mindedly. A sheet fluttered and flew under the bed as Aditi ducked down to grab it.

The telephone was ringing. Did it have to ring right now,

thought Aditi exasperated. She pushed the sheet under the pillow and hurried to take the call. It was Supratim.

"What's up? Were you sitting next to the phone?"

"Not quite. Why?"

"Normally you take so long to pick it up"

"Why did you call?" asked Aditi feeling annoyed at this dilly-dallying.

"What's the mighty hurry? What have you been doing? Cooking? Have you left something on the gas?"

"No."

"I see. I suppose you were writing" Supratim laughed. "Lucky you! Nothing to do except make up yarns."

"Why don't you tell me why you are calling?" Aditi asked impatiently.

Supratim paused. It was for just a few seconds. But they seemed like hours to Aditi. He came to the point, finally.

"Listen, I've got to go to Jamshedpur by the Steel Express this evening."

"Why the sudden need?"

"I've work to do, Madam. Can't make the house run by sitting at home and spinning stories the way you do. My Jamshedpur branch hasn't been able to reach the target and the year ending is fast approaching. I have to go and see if I can retrieve the situation somehow before that. Perhaps I've to think up some new strategies, discount incentive or something else.

Both our boys posted there have turned out big flops. You know who I'm talking about. Pushpal and Samir. Others have also been complaining about them. Well, I simply have to look into it myself ...."

"When are you going to return?"

"Me?" Supratim was taken aback by her sudden interruption, "Tomorrow night, I suppose. I'll ring up if I'm delayed any further."

"Will you come home before leaving for the station?"

"No. That's why I'm calling. There's a lot of work I've to clear up first. I'll go directly to the station from office."

There was nothing new or unusual about Supratim's going. He often went off on small tours directly from the office, though sometimes he came home first. He had gone to Bhubaneswar directly from the office twice last month. It was a routine part of his job. But even then Aditi always worried about him every time it happened. She worried about whether he'd eat something unsuitable and fall sick. Whether his blood pressure would rise alarmingly due to tension. Whether the heat wave would affect him. Whether he'd catch a cold. The worry was not a serious one. It was the kind of anxiety she used to feel for Papai or Tatai after sending them to school when they were young. Such anxiety belonged to the realm of affection rather than romantic love.

But this afternoon none of the anxiety troubled Aditi. On the contrary it filled her with a sense of relief to know that she could get on with her story at night if she couldn't manage to complete it by afternoon. But she said the usual words, "Be careful, won't you?" and added, "May I hang up now?"

"What's the mighty hurry? Here's your poor husband travelling to a distant land and you don't even feel like talking to him, eh?"

Aditi burst out laughing. "Since when has Jamshedpur become a distant land? You've always been dinning into my ears that it's like going to another part of the city and infinitely easier at that."

"Oh well, it isn't home, even if it's so," said Supratim refusing to let go, "What have you been writing today?"

A casual question but Aditi felt happy that he had bothered to ask. "Just a story that I've to read in Hemen Mama's next literary meeting."

"Good. Write away. By the way, who is your victim this time?"

"Victim? What do you mean?"

"Didn't you take it out hard and strong on your brother in your first story? How he cheated his poor unsuspecting sister of her rights and how hurt the sister felt? You did just the right thing, writing about it. Time someone came out with the truth!"

Aditi stood silent. For some reason Supratim was totally convinced that Aditi had written the story of Alakesh and herself. She had failed to explain to him that it was not really so. What she had tried to portray was the basic attachment between siblings that remained despite all odds, a theme as old as time. The relationship often grew bitter when selfishness and self-interest crept in and it looked like the end of things. But in spite of all the apparent bitterness and conflict something remained, something that gushed deep down within one's heart like a hidden spring. Aditi's story had several incidents that were not true of her own life – such as brother and sister flying kites together, the sister holding on to the string. Or the brother giving his marbles to his sister for safe keeping. But despite the differences Supratim found the central theme to be a copy of her own life. So much so, that Aditi herself grew doubtful after a while and could not bring herself to show the story to Tultuli. Even Alakesh had been thrilled to hear that Aditi had started writing once again after all these years and asked to see the story. But Aditi had told him quite glibly that she had lost the magazine. Somehow that had amused Supratim and had convinced him of his belief all the more.

Supratim did not comment on Aditi's silence at the other end of the line and laughed loudly once again. "I like the name you had chosen for your brother in your story – Ramakrishna. So apt! Seeing to his own interests all the time and yet pretending to be indifferent to all worldly matters!"

"Didn't you just say that you have a lot of work to clear before you start for Jamshedpur?" interrupted Aditi in a rude voice.

"Oh, so you mind my speaking the plain truth about your brother, do you? Ha ha! Very well, I shan't say any more. Bye."

Aditi put the receiver down and stood still for a few moments. Then she went to the fridge, took out a bottle of cold water and gulped some down. She also sprinkled some of it on her face and neck. Taking Supratim's call had snapped the thread of her concentration. It would take her quite a while to get back to her story. She walked about the place restlessly and finally went out and stood on the balcony. It was dusk. The rays of the sun tilted backwards getting dimmer by the minute. Evening shadows fell across the grass. A group of girls just back from school stood laughing amongst themselves in a corner of the compound. Shipra's old mother-in-law lay warming her frail body in the glow of the setting sun. The flowers on the Gulmohar tree swayed in the gentle breeze. The parrot was already asleep, its beak tucked away cosily.

Aditi was wrapped up in her story and seemed to feel within her heart all the upheaval felt by her protagonists. She was writing the story of a young couple – Paresh and Asha – who belonged to the lower middle class. They were tired of changing over from one rented apartment to another. Whenever they stayed for more than a year the landlord harassed them by cutting off the water supply. Others bit off their heads if they so much as drove a nail on the wall. Some made nasty comments whenever they returned late. Others simply asked them to pack up and leave. It was a constant shuttle from pillar to post. Bitter and exhausted, the quiet couple were now trying their utmost to find a place of their own. They had approached a promoter hoping to acquire a tiny flat within their means. The promoter, sitting with an Alsatian on either side, had grinned and assured them that he'd find them something within their budget within a year.

Asha and Paresh went all out to find the required money. Paresh took a loan from his office and the cooperative bank while Asha sold off all her jewellery. The construction started. Asha and Paresh ran over to watch its progress whenever they could. As the building gradually took shape they discussed how they would do up their house of dreams. Then out of the blue the construction stopped. Some problem with the corporation. A year went by. Then another. Asha and Paresh grew tense with worry. Finally after two years the work started once again and the young couple started dreaming once more. But this time it was the promoter who shattered their dreams. "It's quite impossible to give you the flat at the rate I had quoted. You have to pay a lakh more. I could arrange a loan for you at 20% interest. You can have the keys of your flat when you've paid back your loan." Asha and Paresh were at their wit's end. How on earth were they to pay any more without actually starving themselves? What could they possibly do to save the situation? Try for more loans? Ask for their money back from the promoter? Return to their bitter existence in rented flats and face the old problems all over again?

Kalyani who lived in the flat next to Aditi's was watering the plants in her balcony. She called out to Aditi. "What's up? I hardly get to see you these days."

Aditi, lost in the problem being faced by Asha and Paresh, did not hear Kalyani.

Kalyani called again, "Are you ill or something?"

Aditi looked at her and shook her head. "I'm OK"

"Papai is getting ready for his part 2, BA, isn't he?"

"Yes."

"When do the exams begin?"

Aditi couldn't remember. What day of the month was it? And what month was it, anyway? It took her quite sometime to return to the present and calculate the date. "Still some time to go. It's from the first week of May."

"Lucky you! Both your boys are nearly grown up. I don't know when my little bounder will do the same."

"Let him complete school next year and you'll see how time flies" said Aditi, smiling.

Kalyani didn't seem to hear her words. Coming close to the grill she asked in a low voice, "Did you hear the commotion in Gopa's flat last night?"

Aditi could vaguely remember some loud voices in the flat below around dinner time. Supratim had made some comment about it. What was it he had said? Ah yes, he had remarked, "There starts the music!" Who had said the words? Was it

Supratim or Tatai?

"What happened?" asked Aditi in a disinterested voice.

"Dear me, haven't you heard? Gopa had been to her husband Siddhartha's office to complain that he no longer gives her any money to run the house. He gives it all to the other woman. You know, the one he's currently having an affair with. She's reputed to be quite a shark."

Kalyani winked at Aditi.

Aditi ignored her invitation and turned her thoughts to her story once again. Even if Asha and Paresh were to ask the promoter to return their money, was he likely to do it? Hadn't Aditi and Supratim faced the very same problem at the time of buying their own flat? The promoter had originally asked for two and a half lakhs and had finally settled for nearly a lakh more. But Supratim had managed to find the money. He had mortgaged two of his insurance policies and taken quite a big loan from his brother-in-law. Didn't Paresh have any relative who could help him out?

Kalyani was not put off by Aditi's lack of enthusiasm and continued to whisper, "All that commotion was because of Gopa's going and complaining."

"She did the right thing," said Aditi thoughtlessly, "Why should she take such things lying down?"

"But do you know who has been encouraging Gopa to do it?" cried Kalyani with redoubled energy, "That fellow who drops in at their flat at all hours. Gopa says it's her cousin but he isn't really. He's the son of her uncle's friend and her husband knows it too."

Kalyani peeped at the flat below and continued to whisper, "Gopa is said to have had an affair with the fellow before she was married to Siddhartha. You can't really expect a husband to put up with his wife's ex-lover running in and out of the house all the time, can you? He is quite justified in having a relationship of his own. You know, my husband was quite enraged when he heard about it. Said if these people continue to behave like slum dwellers we'll sell off our flat and go to live elsewhere. Such a bad example for the children!"

Aditi had never been interested in scandals. She disliked hearing about it now particularly because she was busy trying to think up a conclusion for her story. The doorbell came as a distinct relief as she scuttled away to answer it. It was Malina's mother, back to complete the evening chores. She too had the habit of gossiping whenever she came to work and Aditi listened to her sometimes when she had nothing better to do. But this evening she drove her out the minute her work was done. Her head was beginning to feel heavy. She quickly made herself a cup of tea and sat down with her story once again. Perhaps she would be able to write some more before Sabita came in to cook dinner.

But once again her luck was out. Papai arrived even before Sabita did and was followed by Tatai close on his heels. Papai had his tea and went off to his room for a nap, telling her to wake him up around nine o' clock. Tatai sat down to watch TV. Aditi felt restless. As a rule she loved it when the boys were at home in the evenings. But their presence annoyed and irritated her today. Was it because she wanted to remain undisturbed and get on with her story? It was quite impossible to have any peace or quiet while Tatai was at home. He had the habit of demanding one thing after another.

"Mom, here's some pizza bread. Do make me a cheese pizza."

"Mom, it's such a hot day. Make me a cold drink."

"Mom, don't make it with plain chilled water. Put in some ice cubes as well."

And so it went on and on.

"Where are all your pals today?" Aditi asked him in exasperation, "Don't tell me they have cut you out?"

Tatai burst out laughing. "No, dear Mom, by no means! It's I who gave them the slip because I need a little rest today."

Why today of all days, Aditi asked herself rebelliously, knowing there was no help for it.

At last she was free late at night after the entire locality was still. She closed the door of her bedroom and turned to Asha and Paresh once again. Supposing the promoter returned them their money what would they do? Try and find a smaller, less expensive flat? Was it ever possible for anyone to realise his/her dream completely? What then, was the solution? To cut down one's dream to size? To go for what was within one's grasp?

Her thoughts wandered and she could find no solution. Her story seemed to have gone out of track ever since Supratim's untimely phone call. Aditi put out the light and lay down. But sleep refused to come. She stared aimlessly out of the open window. A tiny storm had been blowing outside cooling down the summer night. But even that didn't bring her any sleep. Aditi felt tired as she looked at the blue darkness outside her window. She simply must find the conclusion to her story! The conclusion ......

Chapter Seven

Hemen arrived around five in the evening just when Aditi was making tea for the family. Her heart had been thudding uncomfortably all day long which increased tenfold at the sight of Hemen. She was about to attend her very first literary meet that evening. The very thought of reading out her story before an august gathering of unknown people made her feet wobble like jelly. What might have seemed an adventure to a 21-year-old seemed an ordeal to a hard boiled housewife of 45. Had she been a fool to agree to Hemen Mama's proposal in a sudden fit of inspiration?

Hemen had dressed up with obvious care that evening. He wore a freshly starched dhoti and kurta and also kolhapuri chappals. He no longer looked like a bent old man. The unusual attire had given him a trim look. Even his face looked younger and less wrinkled. He seemed to be in a hurry.

"What's this, Aditi? Not ready yet?"

"Do I really have to go?" muttered Aditi looking nervous.

"Haven't you been able to complete the story?"

"Yes I have".

"Do you have any special work at home this evening?"

"Not really". She looked helplessly at Supratim. "Why don't you tell him?"

It was a Sunday evening. Supratim was stretched on the sofa sipping his tea leisurely. He put his feet down at the sight of Hemen and said, "Your niece has been whining away all morning, oh dear me, what shall I do, what if they eat me up....and so on..."

"When did I say that?" Aditi protested. "But it is true that I'm nervous. I've been nothing but a housewife all these years. I've never been anywhere except to the houses of friends and relatives. A literary meet sounds scary!"

"Too late, my dear," remarked Supratim, "Now that you're determined to become a writer you have to face such gatherings. Rule of the game. Every profession has its own rules."

Supratim gulped down the last few drops and laid the empty cup on the table.

"You know, Uncle, when I first became a salesman I knew absolutely nothing about how to go about it. Mine was a small company and I had no professional training. I almost funked it. Just then I got to know some others who had been in the same line for quite a while. We got together every evening. Whatever I know now was picked up at those meetings. That's where I collected all my professional tips. One just has to socialise with others if one aims at making it high. Give and take. Teach and learn. Isn't that so, Uncle?"

Supratim's tone carried such obvious authority that it was difficult to contradict him. He was quite equal to convincing his listeners that there was no basic difference between selling soap, oil and stories.

Hemen smiled over his cup of tea. "Aditi, you should be proud of having such an enthusiastic and encouraging husband. I'm sure he must be a great source of inspiration."

"Now you are making me feel embarrassed," said Supratim. "I didn't do very much while I wasn't aware of her talent. But now that it's out in the open, why shouldn't I patronise it? After all, not everyone has a writer for a wife. You know, a friend of mine and his wife wanted to visit us this evening but I said no to him. Told him point blank not to come today as my wife was going to a literary meet."

"And you aren't even ready yet," said Hemen Mama. "Hurry up, we must reach there by six."

Aditi went to her bedroom and sat before the dressing table. Supratim was really a simple and large hearted man with no malice and complications about him, she felt. He wasn't narrow-minded either. Though he teased her about her writing and for taking it up at this age he was really proud of her achievement and made it a point of telling his friends. Kasturi and her husband had dropped in at their place last Sunday.

Supratim had not only told them about her writing but also made them read her story. She remembered how proudly he had told them, "My wife doesn't idle away her time just because our sons are grown up. Just see what a fine pastime she has picked up."

She could hear Supratim talking loudly to Hemen Mama and Hemen answering him back. She couldn't make out what they were talking about. When they got together they didn't stick to any fixed subject for long and changed topics constantly. But it was always Supratim who did most of the talking.

Aditi made up her face with a light hand. She could not stand heat and already had a few heat rashes on her face. Powdering her face lightly she stuck on a small red bindi. Then she called Supratim inside.

"What is it?" asked Supratim taking his own time coming in.

Aditi said, "Why don't you come along with us too?"

"Me? What on earth shall I do there?"

"You'd get to meet a lot of new people. What are you going to do all by yourself at home?" Aditi gave him a straight look, "I'll feel better if you're there too."

"Can't you trust your uncle?" Supratim asked laughing.

"It's not that. But if you're there as well..."

"Can't be done, my dear. Going to literary meets is not my cup of tea. I'll go and look up Deepak instead. When are you likely to return?"

"Whenever Hemen Mama chooses to bring me back."

"Don't be too late. Papai and Tatai will be home soon and I may not be back by then. Don't wait for a bus. Take a taxi. Both ways. Do you have enough with you or shall I give you some more money?"

"I have enough." Aditi hesitated, "I don't think Hemen Mama is likely to let me pay, though".

Supratim peeped out of the door. Hemen Mama was deep in the editorial of the Bengali newspaper.

Supratim turned to Aditi, laughed and said, "No, no don't let him do that. After all he is a retired person. Besides, the niece is perfectly capable of paying for the trip. Also ..."

"Also what?"

"Men have a lot of secrets about which you know nothing. Well-dressed men seldom carry much cash with them. He's more likely to be delighted if you offer to pay."

"How you love to tease," said Aditi opening her wardrobe. "Which of these should I wear?"

"Wear that bottle green Kalakshetram".

"Silk in summer! Besides, it's far too showy, more suited to a wedding reception."

"So what? After all, you are going there for the first time and should look well turned out. Stun your audience with your glamorous looks!"

"No need to stun them when I don't even know how they are going to react to my story."

Aditi pulled out a white handloom sari. "It's a blazing hot day. I'd better dress simply."

Supratim turned up his nose. "Why do you want to look like a nun?"

"Dressing up as a nun is far more suited to my age. I don't need to look like Radha going on a tryst."

"Since you're determined to have it your own way, why ask me?"

Supratim was about to go out of the room when Aditi called him back.

"Why this sudden visit to Deepak?"

"May as well. The poor chap's brooding all alone."

"Has Sharmila left him for good then?" Aditi asked draping the sari around her.

"Looks like it".

"Does the son come to see him?"

"Therein lies the problem. Sharmila doesn't let the child see him. Didn't you hear Somen say how angry he feels about it?"

"Yes and that's why he boozes away to glory".

"A man must have something to turn to. He can't go round whining from door to door, can he? Sharmila will learn her lesson when he takes her to court. Let's see what happens to her adamant attitude then."

Aditi found it difficult to think of a simple, quiet girl like Sharmila being unduly adamant. But this was no time to think of Sharmila. It was Supratim she was worried about.

"Don't you try to play Chunilal just because Deepak has turned into a Devdas", said Aditi tucking in the pleats.

Supratim burst out laughing. "Deepak is quite capable of being a Devdas on his own. He doesn't need any Chunilal to help him."

"I hope you see my point," said Aditi with a serious face.

"I do. I understand what you mean if you so much as open your lips."

"Then remember my words and don't start drinking the moment you land up there."

Supratim felt annoyed. "Can't imagine what you take me for. I have quite a collection of drinks at home. My sons are now old enough not to mind such things. But despite all that, do you find me drinking every evening?"

Aditi held her tongue. Let him please himself, she told herself.

It was his health that worried her. Last year he had been laid up with chest pain for a whole week because he had ignored the doctor's orders.

"You don't have a major heart problem, Mr. Mazumdar," the doctor had told him, "But at your age you just have to cut down on your smoking and drinking."

As a rule Supratim seldom crossed limits. Nor did he drink regularly. But sometimes he did lose control and had a drop too much. Anyway, she couldn't keep nagging him all the time.

There were a few scattered clouds in the sky. Yesterday had been cloudy too, though it didn't rain. The setting sun, though dimmer, continued to send out scorching rays. The concrete jungle with its tar, bricks and iron radiated heat. Usually a cool breeze blew from the south after sundown. But it was too early for that.

The literary meet came as a shock to Aditi. It was nothing like the enormous gathering she had imagined. Just a drawing room in an old two-storeyed house behind the Charu Market. A carpet was spread across the floor where about ten or twelve people sat in small groups talking amongst themselves. Not a single famous writer was in sight. They looked more like the elderly group of superannuated people who chatted by the lakeside to while away their time. There were just a couple of young men rushing around, going in and out of the room. Hemen Mama had told her that it would be a small group but this was no more than a mini drawing room gathering!

Hemen introduced her to the rest. They were mostly school and college teachers or retired librarians. One was a retired judge. Another, the owner of a drugstore. Some of them had already read Aditi's first story and said a few words of praise when Aditi was introduced. One of them said that he had expected the writer to be much older. Another looked disappointed because he was obviously expecting a much younger woman. An elderly lady, one of the ladies of this house, took her by the hand and found her a seat. She had also read Aditi's story. She made detailed enquiries about Aditi's husband and sons. She also told her that two more ladies, both of them teachers, were also expected to arrive.

Aditi lost her uneasiness as she listened to the talk around her. Hemen Mama was the centre of the elderly group. Obviously popular among them, he discussed his own magazine with gusto. Popular writers were mentioned along with the current state of literary movements, concerned because the younger generation hardly ever read books in Bengali. Others spoke of the harmful effects of television. Aditi sat in a corner listening to them. An elderly librarian moved out of his group and came to sit beside her.

"How do you like our literary group?" he asked her.

"Looks quite interesting," said Aditi with a smile.

"Far more homely than other literary clubs, isn't it?"

It reminded Aditi of a vegetable vendor praising his own pumpkins.

"Yes, very homely", she agreed.

"That's what Premtosh had always wanted it to be. The setting should be homely but the discussions sharp. That's what helps bring about the right literary atmosphere. We here believe in being frank. Everyone is free to speak his or her mind."

Aditi had heard about Premtosh from Hemen Mama. A man in his 90s but still pretty tough and active. A kaviraj by profession, he continued to see his patients every morning and evening. But his heart was wholly given to literature. Though he was not a writer himself he was a good critic. He was the owner of this house.

"He isn't here yet, is he?" asked Aditi.

"No he's still upstairs. He'll come down presently. His wife is very ill. Hence the delay."

"What's wrong with her?"

"Cancer."

Cancer! Aditi was stunned. Hemen Mama had never mentioned it to her though he had said that she wasn't keeping too well. But cancer! And all the noise and excitement of a meeting while the lady of the house lay critically ill!

"Don't be surprised", said the librarian, "If a literary meet is scheduled to be held here it's not likely to be cancelled even if the heavens fall down. Didn't you see Anima, Premtosh's daughter-in-law? She is the one that keeps shuttling between her mother-in-law and the meeting. She is also a great lover of literature. Writes reviews for many important literary magazines. And letters to the editors of many newspapers. She teaches English in a college but I think she's due to retire some time this year."

Aditi felt thoroughly confused. Each member of this gathering seemed to belong to a different world.

"Do you write too?" she asked the librarian.

"Oh no. I'm no writer. Most people present here are merely readers. But we all love literature. We often have writers visiting us. Sometimes we ask the famous ones too. Some accept our invitation. Others don't. Do you know how old our club is?"

"I've heard Hemen Mama say it's quite an old one."

"Ancient would be the right word! It has been going strong for almost 40 odd years. We have a meeting once every two months. A lot of famous people have been to our meets in the past. Premendra Mitra, Shailajananda, Achintya Kumar Sengupta, Tarashankar Bandopadhyay and Pramatha Nath Bishi. The club went through a wobbly patch in between. But Hemen's return to Calcutta has given it a new lease of life." Aditi glanced at Hemen reading something out from his magazine to a couple of school teachers.

"Yes, Hemen Mama is a real lover of literature," said Aditi with a smile.

"It's a pity he gave up writing himself. His novel *The Pilgrim* used to be really popular. I remember issuing it regularly in my own library."

Aditi remembered the title. Perhaps there was a copy of the book in their house at Amherst Street. She too had wondered at times why Hemen Mama had given up writing and remembered asking him about it once or twice. But he had never given her a convincing answer and had changed the subject jokingly. She decided to make yet another attempt, a serious one, to find out the reason.

Premtosh came downstairs with Anima, a smile of welcome on his lips. Aditi sat up straight. It must need a very deep love of literature to be able to smile like this on the face of a family disaster! How did one acquire a love like that? It was not prompted by the desire to see one's name in print. Nor the desire for publicity. What, then, made these people gather like this month after month to discuss literature?

Supratim, Papai and Tatai would call them crazy, utterly crazy.

Premtosh leaned on a short, round cushion. He still looked enviably fit. No one would take him to be more than seventy or so. He had a pitch dark complexion and snow white hair. Despite the inevitable looseness of skin he walked erectly with firm, steady steps. Anima looked far older by comparison. Premtosh didn't look old enough to be her father-in-law.

All meetings had to have a chairperson. Premtosh was probably the permanent one. But even then Hemen Mama formally proposed his name, duly seconded by another member. Anima wrote down the minutes of the meeting and got it signed by everyone. The meeting started. Two people had been scheduled to read out their stories that evening. Anil Gupta and Aditi Mazumdar. Anil was one of the two young men. He was the first to read out his story. It had a rather complicated plot that sounded even worse in his lifeless style of reading. Aditi couldn't quite make out what he was trying to get at. Everyone discussed the story after it was read out, rather like a debate. Taking the strong points and the weak points into account, it was passed as a good effort on the whole.

It was Aditi's turn next. She took out her story from her handbag with hands that shook a little. Her heart started beating faster all of a sudden. Her mouth felt dry and her tongue uncomfortably rough. For the first time in her life she was facing a group of listeners who had nothing else to do at the moment. All of them were waiting just to hear her story. Aditi read it out without halting. In her story Asha and Paresh had eventually shifted to another rented flat, larger than their last one. The rent was higher. But there no water problem. It was bigger than what their dream flat might have been, Asha tells Paresh at the end of the story. But Paresh is silent as he asks himself, "Can we really fit in here, Asha? Is there ever a place in this world large enough to hold a person and his dreams, no matter how hard we try to find it?"

But the conclusion sounded somewhat flat and there was hardly any discussion worth the name. Just a few trivial, inane comments. One of the listeners said it was rather weak, specially when compared to Aditi's first story. Asha and Paresh's yearning for a home had not come through convincingly enough. Both Premtosh and Anima felt that though the language was lucid Aditi should have handled the theme better. Hemen said nothing at all. Aditi felt really gloomy. Tea and biscuits were served after the session ended but Aditi was too depressed to have any. She had tried so hard to write the story, snatching at every spare minute like a miser .... And yet it had all been to no purpose! No good at all! She remained silent even after they came out of the house. She didn't even seem to feel the touch of the cool breeze outside. She sweated profusely and her ears burnt in humiliation. It was Hemen who spoke first.

"Do you feel depressed, Aditi?"

Aditi took a small breath but didn't reply to his question.

"One can't be successful every time, you know. It is the attempt that really matters and I know that you had really tried your best. Am I right?"

Aditi nodded silently.

She could suddenly feel a strong determination rising within her. The determination to break up the old Aditi and cast her in a new mould.

Chapter Eight

A hefty young man with a pair of thick moustaches stood on a stool, his torso draped in a sari. At the other side of the entrance stood a thin, rickety fellow wrapped up in a thick bed cover. Looking at the expression on his face one would imagine that he was standing at the mall in Darjeeling gazing at the Himalayas in the soft winter sun. A middle-aged man stood at the other end of the pavilion, his body covered with ladies' bags of various sizes. He reminded one of Christ crucified. Next to him stood a young boy clapping a pair of slippers like a drum as he called out – Sale, sale, sale, sale! Come on, take it, and grab it while you have the chance .... Here's the last piece going!

It was the summer fair at Gariahat, brimful of people and noise. The sweating young man with rubble of beard on his face called out to Aditi, don't go Boudi, listen to me ... Boudi, do listen to me please!

Aditi hadn't really gone far, just a few steps from where he stood calling. It was difficult to make one's way in the jam-packed crowd consisting almost entirely of women. It was a Sunday and tomorrow would be the last day of the fair. It looked like virtually every woman was out of her home today, resembling a troop of female soldiers out on a rampage. It was difficult to walk or stand still amidst so much pushing and pulling. Aditi found it impossible to remain still.

"Why are you calling me back?" she asked the salesman, "You are not prepared to give it to me at the price I quoted."

"Listen to me for a moment, Boudi. Come this way."

"No point. I'm not going to pay any more than what I said."

"Just ten rupees more?"

"No way."

"Five then?"

"Not even one. You're not the only guy here selling bed sheets."

"Very well, have it your way. I can't argue any more."

Aditi smiled. She rather enjoyed bargaining with these people at the fairs and found their desperate faces really amusing. Some of them were wildly frantic to get rid of their stuff. Others put on a nonchalant air or a look of indifference. Some made the whole place lively with their smart talk and jokes. It was not so much the buying itself as the people she bought from that attracted her. Especially the funny way by which they called back their prospective buyers.

Aditi turned back sweating as she struggled to make her way amidst the crowd. But the salesman changed his tone the moment she returned.

"You must pay me five rupees more", he said folding up the sheet neatly.

"Why?"

"Didn't you see how our trade suffered the last two days because of the untimely storm?"

"Rubbish," said Aditi with a frown, "The storm came on in the late evening, long after you people closed shop."

"We don't close that early on the last day or two. The loss of a single evening is like sinking into a manhole. Please Boudi, just five rupees more."

Aditi couldn't but laugh at his clever pleading.

"You are not keeping your word, you know. I don't care to buy things from people who do that."

The boy stuck out his tongue and touched both his ears in a posture of repentance.

"I am asking for the extra fiver because you are an old customer. How can I possibly cheat you? Why don't you consider it a gift of affection bestowed upon a poor brother-in-law?"

Really the boy was too smart for words. Knew just the right words for getting round a simple housewife, talking of affection and all that bunk! Old customer indeed! Aditi could not even remember having seen him before. He was adept at using just the right language to lure customers into buying things from him. It was fortunate that Supratim didn't have to deal with such roadside hawkers. His smart salesmanship would be no match against the tricks employed by these people.

Paper has become rare in today's world of buying and selling. We now live in an era of polythene. Everything is sold in polywraps – from shoes to snacks. The salesman stuffed the bed sheets in a flimsy polybag. Aditi transferred it inside her big shopper. There were petty shoplifters all over the place equally adept at swiping parcels and she still had a lot of shopping to do. It was during these annual sales and fairs that she picked up clothes meant for house wear. Kurtas and pyjamas for her husband and sons and also all their undergarments for the entire year. The boys had no time for buying anything other than fancy clothes meant for casual wear. Supratim always wore superfine kurtas during summer. Aditi still needed to buy those. Both her domestic helps had also told her that they wanted printed saris the New Year. Saris that were superfine but not flimsy. And yes, she also needed to buy pillow covers and a few coffee mugs. Should she go for a couple of printed saris for herself? Well, she told herself, she would if she had the time to buy them after she got through all the essentials.

It was no easy task to buy such a variety of things in a single afternoon. Previously she had always done it in three or four instalments, buying just one kind each afternoon. She spent the rest of the time just looking around. Oh well, those were the days when she had all the time in the world. But now she had a hundred characters crowded in her consciousness clamouring for expression whenever it was afternoon. And she could not neglect her routine chores altogether. Besides, there was nobody else to do them. So she had no choice.

A fat, matronly lady stood arguing with the salesman in a corner. Aditi could not hear what it was all about but she couldn't help feeling amused by the way the lady went about it, one hand on her hip and the other virtually touching the salesman's nose as she screamed, "Don't you dare speak to me like that! You can't force me to take a defective piece. I simply won't take no for an answer."

Aditi could not see the lady's face but she seemed to recognise her style of quarrelling. A vague memory sent its signals across what seemed to be a thousand years as a face took shape in the radar of her mind. A time capsule rose from the depths of the earth and opened before her eyes. Who was it that quarrelled in exactly the same style in school?

Sujata! Aditi shouted, "Hi Sujata!"

The lady turned her head in surprise staring at Aditi's face in wonder, followed by a flash of sudden recognition. Anger disappeared, replaced by unmixed joy and wonder.

"Aditi, isn't it?"

Aditi nodded. A moment's pause and Sujata grabbed her by the hand.

"After such a long, long time!"

"Twenty six years! No, I think it must be twenty eight," said Aditi turning over the pages of her mental calendar.

"How did you manage to spot me in this crowd?"

"I didn't. I merely heard you", Aditi said laughing. Not the carefree laughter of youth but the misty laughter of autumn years.

Looking at Sujata with the eyes of a connoisseur she remarked, "You look quite different. You have put on weight and wear glasses now. But your voice hasn't changed. Nor your style of quarrelling with people!"

"Well, I could hardly help quarrelling this time. The fellow had told me that he would change the sari if it had marks on it and now..."

"You can't change things bought in a sale, Aunty. Anyway, the sari costs just 70 bucks. Wear it for seven days and then throw it away," remarked the skinny salesman.

Sujata glared at him. If looks could kill he'd be dead by now. But since it couldn't she gave up.

"I'll let you off this time but don't you dare cheat anyone else like this in future."

Aditi couldn't shift her gaze from Sujata. The slim and trim oval-faced schoolgirl of yesteryears was now a matronly housewife. Her hair had thinned exposing a broad forehead. Her sideburns were streaked with silver. The eyes under the glasses looked puffy. There were visible rings around her neck. Had 28 years also changed Aditi to the same extent? The face she looked at in the mirror every morning didn't seem so very different to her. Or perhaps it did, without her being aware of it. The change was so gradual that even her own reflection couldn't point its finger at what exactly had changed. The same was true of her near and dear ones whom she saw every day. She must look the same in their eyes just as they did in hers. Time stood virtually still where she and they were concerned. Time seemed to call out and say, I am the same – the same as I had been at 15, 25 or at 45. But supposing she never bothered to look at a mirror and then suddenly looked at one after 30 long years, would she feel the way she now felt looking at Sujata after all these years? Who knew!

Sujata seemed to read Aditi's thought as she tapped her on the shoulder, saying, "You haven't changed much. At least nothing to write home about. What's the secret, eh?"

"No secret at all. I've been looking after my home and running after my two unruly boys – where's the time to put on weight?"

"Well, I don't run around any less than you do – managing home, office, bringing up my children and attending to my husband's needs at one and the same time."

"Are you really working? Where?"

"The Railway. At Fairly Place. What about you?"

"Jail. At Husband's Place. A poor prisoner for life."

The two old friends forgot their advanced years and giggled like two schoolgirls.

"I feel quite jealous of you, staying so trim despite remaining a housewife and here am I ...."

"Do you remember how you laughed at fat girls when we were in school? Remember our tubby Kajal whom you called a pumpkin?"

"I'm not all that fat," protested Sujata. Then she added in a different tone, "You can't imagine how thin Kajal has now become. I met her at the Expo last year and she looked a regular skinnigallee."

"She lost her husband, didn't she? Was it a heart attack?"

"Yes. Isn't it tragic? Do you remember Dipti?"

The two friends chattered non-stop touching upon the past and present. They caught up on virtually all the news about each other in just a few minutes. Which year Aditi had bought her flat. When Sujata built her house at Kasba. About Sujata's son Tablu being in the College of Engineering and her daughter Munia preparing for her Higher Secondary exam the next year. How often Supratim toured outside and just how long he was able to stay home. All the different branches of the bank Sujata's husband had worked in all these years. How important he was because of his position in the Bank Union. What dishes Papai and Tatai disliked and what dishes Tablu and Munia had no use for. Facts went to and fro at record speed and yet they had so much more to catch up on.

It had rained heavily the previous night. The streets were still full of slush. But the sun was blazing down today as it sent heat waves across the western sky and burnt into the skin. The two friends sat facing each other across a small table in a tiny roadside cafe. Aditi picked up the salt cellar from the table and shook it gently. Sujata picked up the pepper jar.

"Have you any news of Manasi?"

"Not really. Haven't met her for years. The last time I saw her was at the Sealdah station when she was doing her MBBS at the N.R.S. Medical College. Probably she was an intern at the time. Swagata told me she married a classmate later on."

"Are you in touch with Swagata then?"

"I see her off and on. She has managed to land a fantastic job in the Reserve Bank. She got in by sitting for an exam and after that there was no looking back. She holds an important post now. She always was lucky."

"Why call it luck? Swagata has always been the most brilliant amongst us all. Always scored marks in the nineties, especially in maths."

"You were no less brilliant. Swagata never could beat you in the languages, English or Bengali. And you wrote such lovely stories and poems."

Aditi's heart skipped a beat. Here was someone who could remember all that she could do even after a gap of 28 years while she herself had completely forgotten about her ability to write. Had she really forgotten? Or had she forced herself to forget? For a moment she felt tempted to tell Sujata that she had taken up writing once again. But she changed her mind the very next moment. She could put up with the indifference of her own family members but it would hurt her no end if her friend felt compelled to praise her efforts without really meaning it.

Aditi sighed and changed the subject.

"You were very good at debates she said", "we always said you'd end up becoming a lawyer."

"And so I did", said Sujata, "I studied law and started practising in the High Court, wearing a full-sleeved blouse and a black gown, a white bow around my neck...."

"But you just told me you work in the railways".

Sujata's voice lost its early enthusiasm. She sounded as dismal as a cloudy evening as she replied, "I was compelled to give up my practise."

"Why? Did you find it too tough?"

"It was tough but that was not the reason I gave it up. Besides, I wasn't doing so badly either. Deepesh Bagchi, my senior, was a great help and had started getting me my own individual cases, but ...."

"But what?"

"I had to give it up after I got married."

"Why? Are your in-laws so conservative?"

"It's difficult to explain. Depends on what you mean by conservatism."

Aditi stared at her, not quite taking in what she meant. Sujata's smile was pathetic.

"It will need quite a lot of explaining. Ours was a love marriage. Bikash has always been keen on unions ever since he joined the bank. So he needed legal advise and often came to meet my senior at court. That's how I met him. You can't imagine how crazy he was about me, a junior woman lawyer. He took to dropping in regularly. Every single day, in fact. He was not in need of legal advise. He just came to see me, went to whichever court I was attending and stood staring at me for hours. He told me that he had never come across such a dashing and pushy girl in his life. Can you imagine where he proposed to me? In the court room of the Chief Justice! Pulling me to a corner of the empty hall he grabbed my hand and said, I swear by this court of law that I cannot live without you!"

"How very romantic!"

"Yes, that's what it sounds like when you hear about it for the first time."

Sujata picked up a piece of cucumber and nibbled at it.

"Well, we got married soon after. My in-laws seemed to be quite thrilled with me at first. My mother-in-law showed off her lawyer daughter-in-law to all her neighbours. My father-in-law told his landlord proudly, 'Now that I've a lawyer for a daughter-in-law, I'm no longer scared of you!' You can't call it being conservative, can you?"

"Then what went wrong?"

"No *then* about it, Aditi. The world hasn't really altered despite superficial changes. Before the year was out my father-in-law started feeling that I was returning home too late from my senior's chamber. My mother-in-law was annoyed because I couldn't help her much with the household chores. It was enough to shatter one's peace of mind."

"What about your husband?"

"He didn't make any comments one way or the other. After all, he was a union leader, well grounded in tact. But I could clearly feel that he didn't like it either. It might be wonderful to fall in love with a dashing lawyer but having one for a wife was a different cup of tea altogether. Every man wants his wife to be utterly docile and domesticated. He might enjoy lying in bed and telling her all about his office unions. But the moment she starts telling him about her court cases it feels like lying next to a law textbook. The moment I tried to be logical, either with my husband or his parents, they felt I was talking shop. I got quite fed up ultimately and decided to give it up for good."

"Of your own free will?"

"What else can I call it? If I spent even a little extra time at my senior's, my husband grew livid. My senior got mad if I didn't spend enough time studying the cases and felt I wasn't taking my work seriously enough. In the midst of all this I got pregnant. So giving it all up seemed the only way out."

"When did you pick up your current job?"

"Soon after my son was born. My husband told me, 'what's the use of sitting at home? Find a simple, uncomplicated government job.' I was quite young then. I sat for the exam and qualified for a job. At last there was peace at home, since I had said good bye to all ambition for good."

"Why sound so gloomy? You are working, after all, and also meeting people. What's more, you have an independent existence."

"Independent, my foot! If you're a working woman your feet are chained even more tightly. You have to slog like a dog from the morning – seeing to the cooking, getting lunch ready for husband and daughter, gulping down my own meal and then dashing off to catch a bus amidst all the office rush. It's a blessing my son lives in the hostel or I'd have had to do a thousand and one things for him as well. Even after you land up in office you're terrified of getting late and losing a day and then end up listening to all the comments of your male colleagues. Things like, Can't imagine why women come to work, taking up the place of some needy guy! If they are that keen about running their homes efficiently, why don't they stop home altogether? And as for work, how can you expect them to work when they are dying to get away even before it's four o clock?"

Aditi frowned.

"And you take all these comments lying down, without answering back?"

Sujata laughed. "You are lucky, Aditi. At least you are steadily secure on a single boat. Managing home and office together is like tightrope walking. You need to balance continuously. It's so long since I took up this job but it still feels like being in a circus."

The boy had brought in their tea.

Aditi took out her handkerchief and mopped her face. She couldn't quite make out what exactly Sujata wanted – the life of a housewife or that of a career woman.

"Then why work if it is so much trouble? Why not give it up and remain home peacefully?"

"Good heavens, how can I? My family needs my salary. My husband can't meet the budget on his own."

"In that case he too should help with the household chores. He should realise all you have to go through in office since housework takes up so much of your time."

"He does realise it but doesn't do anything about it. Perhaps he remembers it at the time of addressing his union but forgets all about it the moment he is home. He tells me, 'Oh, so you're back from office. When did you arrive? Get me a cup of tea, won't you? I'm dead tired. Oh, I expect you are tired too. Don't bother about tea then. Bring me a cup of coffee instead'!"

Aditi burst out laughing and nearly choked over her tea.

"He sounds like a carbon-copy of my husband."

"Quite likely. There's just one kind of husband in the world.

All the rest are mere Xerox copies, hundreds and millions of them. One of them gets to become the husband of Aditi. The rest become husbands of all the Sujatas, Manasis, and Swagatas of the world. It's a universal mould. You'll find copies all over the world – in the US, France, Germany, China or even Japan."

"That's a bit too much," said Aditi giving her friend a playful punch. "The man who lives in the flat below ours is always helping his wife with the household chores. When the maid plays hooky, he cuts up the vegetables, does the dusting and even does the dishes."

"Those are the defective copies. Haven't you come across blurred, badly printed photocopies that are no use and have to be thrown away? Those are the few helpful husbands. We also have a few in our office. Everybody jokes about them. We join in too. Call them henpecked husbands." Sujata winked at Aditi. "I am so dead tired of seeing hubby's slaves. Does me good to come across a few henpecked ones. Anyway, I have managed to pull through most of my life like this. Guess I can manage it for another twenty years or more."

Sujata laughed as she said the words. But Aditi could feel a hidden thorn somewhere that just wouldn't stop pricking ...

Aditi threw herself down on the bed like a dead soldier the moment she returned home. Meeting an old friend ought to have cheered her up, making her heart as clear as the bright blue sky. But she felt stray flakes of clouds covering it up. She didn't even feel like getting up and looking at the things she had bought at the fair. Supratim, Papai and Tatai were in the drawing room. They had no interest in her shopping. They were busy arguing, their eyes on the newspaper. Tatai was beginning to get really interested in share markets. Throughout the week father and son discussed the possible rise and fall in shares and eagerly checked who had been more accurate at the end of the week. Supratim was not unduly worried about Tatai's studies or how many textbooks he was reading. But he had quite successfully managed to get him addicted to share markets, something he knew Aditi really detested.

Supratim came into the room after a while to fetch his matchbox. He stopped by to see Aditi lying silently.

"What's up? Why are you in bed at this hour?"

"No particular reason," said Aditi covering her eyes with her hand.

"Do you feel unwell?"

"No."

"Got a headache? It has been a darn hot afternoon."

"How does it matter? You haven't been following me around with a sunshade, have you?"

"So that you might plough the fair even more thoroughly? No, I didn't."

"Ploughing is the right word," said Aditi, "But in this case I had to play a triple role – that of bull, plough and the land."

"Indeed!"

"There's a packet of fish-fry on the table. Better eat it while it's still hot. And please switch off the light."

"What's wrong with you? Thinking of a new plot for your story?" Supratim laughed.

Aditi could have told him, do I think of stories all the time? Who, then, runs your house?

But she knew it was no use telling him. He just wouldn't understand.

The sky outside was overcast with clouds. There were frequent flashes of lightning. A blue flame streaked across the sky. The storm was about to break.

Chapter Nine

"Call for you, Mom," shouted Papai.

Aditi was in the bath. It had been an incredibly hot day. One felt crazy without a cold shower in the evening. Shutting off the shower she called out, "Who is it?"

"Sharmila Aunty."

"Who?"

Aditi was taken by surprise. Why was Sharmila, of all people, calling her up? She had been totally out of touch with Aditi and her crowd of late.

"Will you be out soon or shall I ask her to call up later?" asked Papai.

"Tell her to hold on. I'm just coming."

Aditi didn't bother to rub herself dry and pulled on her clothes on her dripping body. The longer they remained wet the cooler she'd feel. But she dried her hands before picking up the phone.

"Good to hear from you after such a long time. Anything wrong?"

"I've to tell you something important," said Sharmila in a heavy voice.

"Go ahead."

"I can't speak of it over the phone. Could you meet me somewhere?"

"Why not come here?"

"At your place?" Sharmila sounded startled, "It's rather confidential. I don't want anyone else to hear it. When can I find you alone?"

"I'm usually alone in the afternoons."

"Afternoon?" Sharmila sounded worried, "Will you be in tomorrow?"

"I will," said Aditi beginning to feel curious, "How's your son?"

"Fine."

"Are you calling from your parents' place?"

"No, from a public booth. Sharmila paused for a moment. "Please don't tell anyone that I am coming. I mean, don't let Supratim know. Please."

Aditi put the receiver down, lost in thoughts. How could she possibly help to sort Sharmila's personal problems? As far as she knew Sharmila and Deepak had already taken the matter to court. And why was she so insistent about not telling

Supratim? Could there be something going on between the two of them? No, that was absurd! She felt surprised at herself for having thought of such a thing after being married to Supratim for more than 23 years. She knew him as well as the back of her hand. They had been to a thousand and one parties with Deepak and Sharmila. The two families had even travelled to Dehradun and Mussoorie together eight years ago. She had never seen Supratim show any improper attention to Sharmila. On the contrary he always maintained a certain distance from the wives of all his friends. Of course he teased them and joked with them but always within limits. Everyone knew it and admired his ability to conform to it at all times. Did Sharmila want to make it up with Deepak and wanted Aditi to mediate between them? But why hide it from Supratim? Was she ashamed to let the world know that she wanted to return to her husband? Perhaps that was it.

Anyway, there was no point bothering about her imaginary assumptions. She had a lot of things on her hands. Papai was in the midst of his exams and needed special attention all through the day and even at night. He refused to have a proper meal at any time saying that a full stomach made him sleepy. But on the other hand, he couldn't concentrate if he was hungry. So he kept nibbling at things as long as he was awake and Aditi had to provide them. A milkshake at 7 pm. Mangoes at 8 pm. The fruit had to be cut up into bite-size pieces and cooled in the fridge an hour before he had them or they wouldn't taste right. In between eating his friends dropped in or he rushed to some friend returning breathless with a sheaf of notes. "Please, Mom, get these xeroxed right away."

When his exams were on Aditi had no time to think of her own writing, let alone solve riddles about what Sharmila wanted. It wasn't particularly difficult to keep herself from mentioning it to Supratim. She'd wait and see what exactly Sharmila wanted before she spoke about it.

Sharmila arrived braving the scalding summer noon. It was the last day of Papai's exams. The maids had not arrived for their evening chores as yet. The house was really empty. Sharmila came in, her face flushed red in the sun and perspiring profusely. She spoke out what she had come to say without any preamble. Supratim had been to her parents' house with Deepak while Sharmila was away and had actually threatened to expose her as an adulteress in court if she didn't give up the custody of her son. And that was not all. Both of them had also been to Tintin's school more than once. Deepak had said a lot of dirty things about her to the principal. They had even tried to bring away Tintin from school by force one day. Sharmila knew from experience how low a man like Deepak could stoop to get his own end and had not been unduly surprised. But she could not understand Supratim's involvement in the matter.

Aditi felt thunderstruck after hearing Sharmila. It seemed incredible that Supratim had not mentioned the matter to her. And it was equally difficult to believe that a mature man of

Supratim's years could actually behave in such a childish manner. Here was a woman almost accusing Supratim of aiding and abetting in the kidnapping of her son and Aditi was obliged to take it lying down. What embarrassment!

"Why are you telling me all this?" Aditi asked in a dry voice, "Why didn't you speak to Supratim directly?"

Sharmila took a long breath.

"I didn't dare to! He and Deepak are such close buddies. I thought I'd tell you first. You are a woman after all. You ought to understand what I'm going through."

Aditi touched her shoulder.

"Relax. So you didn't go to office today?"

"No, I came here straight from home."

"You are panting. I'll get you a cold drink."

Sharmila took a sip or two and laid the glass on the table.

"I guess you hated hearing about it."

Aditi herself could not analyse what she felt actually. Anger? Humiliation? Insult?

She tried to keep her voice level as she answered, "I don't know how deeply my husband is involved in your affairs. If he has really played an active role it was wrong of him to have done it. But tell me this, why did Deepak start feeling so mad with you all of a sudden? After twenty long years of marriage?"

"It is difficult for an outsider to realise the actual relationship that exists between a husband and a wife. Especially in an ordinary, civilised family like ours. As a matter of fact, it is not something that erupted all of a sudden. Deepak has always been like this."

"Then why didn't you terminate the marriage as soon as you realised it instead of waiting for all these years?"

"We women don't like the thought of breaking up unless we are driven to it. We always feel like giving it another chance, thinking we ought to mend the holes in the relationship somehow and go on. When I didn't get pregnant soon after marriage he drove me crazy and blamed me bitterly for it. You don't want a baby because you think it's going to ruin your figure! You are far too proud of your looks! One day he actually threw a glass at me missing my eye by inches. He'd get into a rage first and then burst into tears afterwards. When I got pregnant at last after eight long years I thought that our trouble was at an end. But I was wrong. That's when he started suspecting me of being unfaithful. 'This baby isn't mine', he kept telling me over and over again."

"What reason could he possibly have to say such a thing?"

"People like Deepak don't go by reason."

"But one can't start suspecting a person of being unfaithful out of the blue," said Aditi giving her an oblique look. "Something must have happened to shatter his faith in you."

Sharmila did not look unduly hurt at the accusation though a deep flush covered her pretty oval face for a moment and disappeared almost instantly. She smiled pathetically at Aditi saying, "Listen Aditi, faith and faithlessness are strange words and mean different things to different people. Faith has a body of its own like birds, beasts or human beings. It can break, grow or die. But suspicion is an airy thing, like smoke or mist. The eye cannot always see it but it hits the very pupil of the eye. And everything looks blurred and out of focus when you try to see with those smokey eyes. You can neither kill the smoke, put it off or blow it out. See what I mean? You don't need any facts to suspect a person. It creeps in like smoke through some tiny chink of our vision. And then we try to look around and find motives to fit the suspicion. If one motive doesn't fit we try to find another. Deepak never had any faith in me to start with. So the question of breaking his faith does not arise. He suspected me when I didn't get pregnant and suspected me when I did. He felt suspicious if I arrived from office early and suspicious if I returned late. Now that I am a mature woman, the mother of a 12-year-old boy, even now he suspects me of having an affair with a 28-year-old colleague. The poor boy has lost his sister and thinks of me as one. But look at me. I have heard so many people saying things about him and Dheera but I have never paid the slightest heed to the remarks. Why should I? I know for certain that Deepak is quite incapable of loving anyone other than himself. And he is incapable of having an affair with Dheera or anyone else. If he did I'd feel sorry for Dheera."

Sharmila had started talking on a quiet note but she grew

thoroughly excited by the time she had completed saying all she had to say. Picking up the glass of cold drink from the table she emptied it in a single gulp. Then she lay limp on the sofa and closed her eyes.

"I see your point," said Aditi, "But do you need to drag poor Tintin into all this?"

"Yes I do. Deepak needs to learn his lesson. He is said to be crying over my boy now but it was he who had refused to believe that Tintin is his child. I know why he wants Tintin's custody. To pay me back. I shall not let him go as long as I live. If he brings five allegations against me I shall bring fifty against him. I have gone through hell all these years. I refuse to take any more. I am no longer afraid of him. Or afraid of what the society might say."

Aditi looked at Sharmila wondering how it had been possible for her to bottle up so much spleen against a man she had lived with for twenty long years. Then what was a relationship all about? Just standing still and spreading out branches, leaves and flowers without the support of a root down below? Or was it really tight rope walking as in a circus?

She brought the matter up that night just before going to bed. Not directly but in a roundabout manner.

"What happened to the case between Deepak and Sharmila?" she asked Supratim.

"They've both gone to court."

"Who did? Deepak or Sharmila?"

"Sharmila. But Deepak intends to fight to the last."

"What's the fight about? Divorce? Doesn't Deepak want to divorce her?"

"It's about the custody of their son. Deepak doesn't want to give him up. The fight's likely to be a long one."

Aditi did not use the mosquito net during summer. Putting a fresh mat in the mosquito-repellent machine she switched it on for the night.

"I think Sharmila ought to get the custody of her son," she remarked.

"Why?"

"Because she's the mother, of course. Children always prefer to remain with their mothers."

"We have to wait and see which side wins."

"I fail to see why Deepak is contesting. How is he going to look after the boy all by himself? He'll hit the bottle the moment it's dark and ruin the poor child's future in the process."

"I fail to see why you should worry about it. It isn't any of our business. Why get involved in what doesn't concern us?"

Supratim put on his glasses. "When do Papai's practicals start?"

"He'll know the dates this Monday."

Aditi looked at Supratim's reflection in the mirror.

"Why do you keep saying that it doesn't concern us? Isn't

Deepak an old friend of yours?"

"I don't see how that matters. It's better for them to part as friends rather than live together as enemies."

"They are bound to remain enemies whether they live together or far from each other," said Aditi.

"I expect you are right. Their relationship had really grown bitter of late," said Supratim, "But why all this sudden concern about them?"

Aditi decided to bring matters to a head.

"Aren't you concerned about them too?"

"Me?"

"Yes. You! Why pretend? Sharmila was here this afternoon. Here are you, giving me philosophical pep talks about staying aloof from other people's affairs while you yourself have been spreading scandals about Sharmila. Aren't you ashamed of yourself? You can't imagine how insulting Sharmila was to me about your involvement in their affairs."

Few people can help getting angry when caught telling a lie. A helpless anger that's all the more intense for that very reason. Supratim took a long puff and then put out his cigarette.

"Why didn't you tell me about Sharmila's visit all this time?"

"You too had never told me about going to Sharmila's parents or going to Tintin's school. Or anything at all about your childish antics."

"Don't talk rubbish. Do you think whatever Sharmila might have told you is the Gospel truth?"

"Then tell me what the truth is. That's all I've wanted to know. Why do you want to hide it from me?"

Supratim gave her the the angry look of a killer cat driven against the wall and took a long breath. Then he gulped down the entire water from the jug, tugged at the bed switch and put out the light.

"I did what I thought to be right." Supratim's voice sounded like a hiss. "Do I have to justify my actions to you?"

Aditi switched on the light promptly.

"Why do you want to darken the room? Are you ashamed to show your face?"

"Will you let me sleep?" Supratim's voice was a shriek now. "I've to slog like a donkey all day to feed the lot of you. I won't put up with scenes at midnight."

Aditi was stunned into silence. Supratim remained silent too. He went about the house next morning wearing the expression of an angry bulldog. He left very early and returned home late. That became the pattern since the fateful night. He disappeared for the whole day on holidays ignoring his need for rest and home comforts. He even stopped talking to the boys. Papai and Tatai had seen their father angry before and left him severely alone. Both turned to Aditi instead.

"What's wrong with Dad? Why is he so badly put off? What did you both fight about this time?"

Aditi made a face and changed the subject hurriedly. What could she possibly tell them?

On previous occasions she had always been the first one to make it up whenever they had a quarrel because she hated seeing Supratim go about the house looking like an angry owl. Although he was pretty go-as-you-please on the whole, there was a streak of obstinacy in him that had to be cajoled back into good humour. But Aditi refused to do it this time. A puff of sizzling air seemed stuck in her chest that simply would not cool. It was quite possible that Supratim had been to Sharmila's house simply to keep Deepak company and at Tintin's school for the very same reason. Deepak was no good at talking. He might have forced Supratim to go with him. And it was perfectly natural on Supratim's part to stand by his friend, even if he was in the wrong. But why did he have to hide it from Aditi? That's what hurt her the most. What was the need to lie about it? And to her, of all people.

Hemen turned up a few days later accompanied by a young man of thirty or thereabouts. He often brought people with him when he came to see her these days. But Aditi had not met this young man before. He was rather attractive to look at. Slim and trim, he had a fair complexion, a smooth beard and large expressive eyes. He wore a soft yellow kurta and white pyjamas and carried a tote bag on his shoulder.

Aditi liked him on sight.

She had been in the kitchen, cooking, and came running out ladle in hand.

Hemen made himself comfortable on the sofa as he said, "Well Ranjan, here is Aditi Mazumdar. She works with the ladle on one hand and the pen on the other."

Aditi gave an embarrassed laugh.

"That's giving me more credit than I deserve. I have written just four stories in all. And as for the ladle, it's because our cook chose to play truant today ...."

"I just loved your story, specially the one called *Cracks*," said Rajan eagerly.

He had a beautiful baritone voice, rather like Hemen Mama's had been when he was young.

Was he also good at elocution?

"I read your next story too," continued Ranjan, "What was its name?"

Aditi laughed. "So you don't remember the name, eh? That means you didn't really like it."

"That's not true. I liked it very much. But there are some stories which go straight to the reader's heart. Your *Cracks* was a story like that. Something I could really identify with. My uncle, who also read the story felt strongly about the tragedy of the theme."

The gnawing depression of the last few days seemed to get lighter by the minute. Aditi smiled again and said, "Well, I can't stand still after facing so many compliments. Tell me, what will you have? Something hot? Or would you prefer a cold drink?"

"Hot of course. A steaming cup of tea, if you don't mind," said Hemen. "Is your elder son through with his exams?"

"Yes, thank goodness. He had the last of the practicals yesterday."

"What exam is it?"

"B. Sc. finals."

Ranjan gave her an incredulous look.

"Really? It seems impossible to believe that you have a grown up son!"

Aditi laughed again.

"Not just one grown up son but two. The younger one will soon be starting his second year of college."

"Believe me, you don't look a day older than thirty-five."

Hemen roared with laughter.

"Aditi, you'd better put some extra sugar in his tea after a compliment like this!"

Aditi hurriedly completed her chores and sat down to have tea with the others. She had already put out a big plate of biscuits, salted snacks and ice cold sandesh.

Hemen sipped his tea as he remarked, "Ranjan is getting to be a very good writer too. Two of his stories have appeared in the *Desh* magazine."

Aditi frowned, trying to remember. "Are you Ranjan Dasgupta by any chance?"

Ranjan scratched his head, a shy smile lurking about his lips, "Well, that's the name my parents chose for me."

"I remember reading both your stories. *Dream Boat* and *The Mathematical Race*. Am I right?"

Ranjan nodded.

"Where do you stay? Somewhere this side?" asked Aditi.

"No, I live in just the opposite direction. In Barasat."

"They have a literary group of young writers at Barasat," added Hemen. "They hold regular sessions of story reading and discussions. Another young writer in their group – Anisur Rahman – is also doing very well. Have you read anything by him, Aditi?"

"The name sounds familiar. I think I have."

"Why not bring him over sometime, Ranjan? Now that you know where Aditi lives."

"Yes, I could." Looking at Aditi he added, "Why don't you visit our group sometime?"

"I am not a young writer," protested Aditi. "I am going to be forty-six this November."

"And how long do you intend to remain forty-six?" Asked

Hemen with laughing eyes.

"What do you mean?"

"They say once a woman turns thirty she has a birthday once every three years."

"You're impossible!" said Aditi doubling up with laughter. "How can I possibly hide my age with two boys as tall as bean stalks?"

"Your age is of no consequence in this case," said Ranjan. "Since you happen to be a new writer you qualify as a young writer too, even if your age happens to be 80. Am I right?" he asked looking at Hemen.

Aditi's heavy heart was beginning to feel light and newly washed with all these random jokes, comments and laughter. Even the hot summer felt pleasant as a soft and gentle breeze blew in through the window. The door of the dream chamber in her heart was starting to open. All this talk of writing and stories were taking the shape of a fairy tale and pushing her back to her golden childhood and youth, which had seemed lost forever.

Hemen tapped his feet on the floor.

"Have you written anything lately, Aditi? Haven't had a story from you for a long time."

Aditi smiled self consciously.

"I'd been working on one before Papai's exams started. It isn't quite ready yet. I'll give it to you later."

"Why later? Why not today?" Ranjan's voice was eager.

"Bring it and read it out to us right away," said Hemen. "Ranjan has to go back all the way to Barasat."

"It's not really ready for reading out. I have to rewrite some parts."

"You are behaving just like my young sister. She has a beautiful voice but whenever anyone asks her to sing she says, my voice is quite ruined after eating too many ice creams."

Eventually Aditi was compelled to fetch her story and read it out. But before she could complete reading a page or two Tatai dashed into the room. His face fell at the sight of the guests.

"What's wrong, little master? Why do you look so glum?" asked Hemen.

"Why haven't you switched on the TV?" he asked with a wooden smile. "There's a match on between Brazil and Argentina. A live telecast."

"So there is," said Ranjan looking at his watch, "Supposed to start at eight, isn't it?"

"Wouldn't you like to see it?" Tatai cried eagerly.

"I wouldn't mind. But we are listening to your mother's story right now."

Tatai looked at his mother. "You could hear it after the match, couldn't you?"

"Oh no, I'll get very late if I wait that long. I'll see the repeat telecast tomorrow morning."

Tatai looked like it was the end of the world as he slumped into the sofa and fidgeted aimlessly. He picked up nuts from the plate and munched steadily looking disturbed. Hemen felt sorry for him.

"Can't we sit somewhere else and listen to your story, Aditi? Then the little master can watch the game in peace."

Aditi thought for a moment. She could take them to the boys' room. But Papai was likely to be in any moment now and would want to be there. She decided to take them to her own bedroom.

Hemen sat comfortably on one side of the bed, Ranjan next to him. Aditi sat on the other side, facing them as she read out her story. She heard Supratim come in, stand by the door for a while, a polite smile on his face as he looked at Hemen. Then he moved into the drawing room and sat watching television with his son.

Ranjan was completely bowled over by the story. Hemen was less vocal. He felt that Aditi should rework on some of the parts. He felt that the reaction of the heroine after meeting her long lost friend should have been handled with far more intensity and depth. But Ranjan wanted Aditi to send it to an important magazine right away. He felt that the story was perfect just as it was and needed no further rewriting. The simple conclusion of the story was heart warming. They took quite a while discussing the story at length. By the time they left it was already half past nine.

Aditi laid the table for dinner treading on cloud nine. It was Supratim who shattered the spell.

"I'd like to know what all this means," he exploded ignoring the presence of both his sons. "Why should every Tom, Dick and Harry intrude the privacy of my bedroom?"

Aditi was stunned by the sudden accusation.

"I took them there to read out my story because Tatai was watching the TV in the drawing room. I didn't think you'd mind since Hemen Mama is practically a family member."

"I don't care what you think! And what about that bearded, soppy-looking fellow? Is he a family member too?"

Aditi felt angry about the unfair accusation.

"Are they the first strangers to enter our bedroom? What about your own gang of friends – Saumen, Tathagata and others? Do they sit in the drawing room all the time when they are visiting?"

"How dare you compare my friends to these unknown busybodies? there should be a limit to all things! Don't you ever dare to bring in strangers in my bedroom again!"

Aditi turned crimson at the insult and implications. They had had many tiffs before on family matters. It had not always been possible to hide them from Papai and Tatai in a flat as small as theirs. But the language used by Supratim tonight was the absolute limit. How could he behave in such a petty manner for something so simple and casual? Could a well known person really turn into an unknown monster at a moment's notice?

But Aditi gulped down her humiliation and served dinner to her boys. And also Supratim. The boys looked grim and ate silently. Supratim tucked in with his usual gusto as though nothing had happened. He tapped the round bone of the meat noisily on the steel plate and sucked the marrow noisily. Then he went on to eat the mango, licking the inner seed white with obvious relish. Aditi lay silent in bed after dinner. A choking heat wave raged outside. It was equally stuffy and hot inside. Bodies were bathed in sweat despite the fan whirling overhead. Supratim turned off the light and touched Aditi.

"Hey!"

Aditi lay silent and unresponsive like a block of wood.

"Are you still mad with me?"

Aditi grew stiffer.

He brought his face close to hers. A familiar breath, hot and intense, touched her face.

"Don't be mad any more," said Supratim in a soft voice. "Remember how you had insulted me the other night? I merely paid you back in your own coin tonight. So we are quits now."

Aditi's blood stopped flowing for an instant. Was Supratim crazy? How could he compare his own deception with her simple thoughtlessness? Could it really be the same Supratim?

Even after a period of twenty-three long years why did his intimately-known presence appear to be so unfamiliar? Aditi broke away from his embrace.

"Go to sleep," she said in a broken voice and turned over to the other side.

Chapter Ten

Aditi shuddered at the sight that met her eyes when she went to feed the parrot in the morning a few days later. The balcony was full of tiny green feathers. The cloth with which she covered the cage at night lay on the floor. The parrot lay limp in a corner of the cage, a deep wound on its left wing. Dark blood clots covered the rest of its green body. Was the parrot dead?

Aditi's relationship with Supratim was still far from normal. Neither spoke to one another unless forced to. Even when they did, it was always in the passive voice.

Sometimes Supratim would shout, "My socks?"

"Behind the shelf," Aditi would shout back.

Or Supratim would ask, "When will dinner be served?"

"When people are seated at the table," Aditi would answer.

Sometimes questions were asked through the boys.

"Tatai please ask your father if he will go to your aunt's place directly from the office or come home first."

"Papai, please remind your mother that the day after is Rinki's birthday so we have to decide tomorrow what to take."

Very often an unexpected calamity helps to clear the air and turn things to normal once again.

Forgetting all resentment Aditi now rushed to Supratim with a wild cry. "Please come and see what has happened to my bird."

Supratim rubbed his sleepy eyes and hurried to see what the matter was. He looked equally bewildered at the sight that met his eyes.

Aditi grabbed his arm without even being aware of it and trembled like a child.

"What shall I do? Will my parrot die?"

Supratim bent his head and looked at the bird carefully. Then he said in the tone of a responsible guardian, "Don't lose your head. We'll have to do something about it."

"What can we do?"

Supratim opened the door of the cage and was about to touch the bird but he stopped midway.

"It is badly wounded. How did it happen?"

"I can't imagine," said Aditi bursting into tears. "Please do something."

"This is the problem of keeping a bird as a pet," said Supratim. "I had told you so many times to keep an Alsatian or a Doberman. No one would have dared to come near them. But you would have a bird! Now go and fetch me a clean towel."

Aditi rushed to get one. She also fetched Papai and Tatai.

Supratim lifted the wounded bird on the towel with great care and scrutinized the wound. The parrot lay very still, almost like one dead. It made no sound at all although it opened its eyes once or twice.

Papai said, "It's done for. Look, this must be its last breath."

"Oh no, it will live," said Tatai, "It's only the wing that has been really injured."

"For a bird the wing is the most important part of its being."

"I don't think so. A wingless bird can live even if cannot fly. The vital parts are the heart, lungs, brain and abdomen. Those haven't been hurt."

"Still a wingless bird is as good as dead."

"Stop arguing and help me, you two," said Supratim. "There's a tube of antiseptic cream produced by my company on your mother's dressing table. Go, fetch it pronto."

"Shouldn't you first wash the wound with Dettol, Dad?"

"Don't, Dad. Dettol stings like fury. Wash it with hot water instead."

"Our cream does not require prior washing. Aditi, you go and get it."

Aditi rushed out and soon returned with the tube of cream.

The parrot was now the focus of attention. Father and sons stood tending its wounds, talking nineteen to the dozen. Medicine is something about which every layman claims to know a great deal, though nobody ever agrees with another. If one says, bandage it up, the other says, no, no, the wound ought to remain open.

Papai said, "Give it anti-biotic in small doses."

"A pain-killer would do far more good," said Tatai.

Both boys felt the bird should be taken to a vet.

Supratim felt sure that he was quite equal to handling it on his own. His cream was bound to do the trick and heal up the wound in no time. But he decided to feed the bird some iron tonic with a dropper to help make up its loss of blood.

Everyone appeared to be an expert on bird care and spoke out his mind.

Papai looked at the grill of their balcony with eyes like Hercule Poirot.

"How could a cat get in through such tiny gaps? It must have been inside the house somewhere, hidden and waiting."

"Don't be silly," said Tatai. "If it had been inside how could it go outside once again without leaving any trace? It couldn't have unbolted the balcony door by itself, could it? A cat has a very flexible body. It must have squeezed in through the grill somehow."

"The foolish bird must have been asleep," added Supratim,

"Or it would have let out a screech or two when the cat attacked it."

"How could it attack from outside the cage?"

"The bird must have been leaning on the cage and the cat got its paw on to it somehow. They can attack real fast. In fact they are the fastest moving creatures among domestic animals."

"And the most wicked as well. Absolutely treacherous. Try bringing up a kitten on fish, milk and what have you, but you will find it emptying out your own kitchen at the first opportunity. They're the most desperate of creatures."

Aditi listened to their comments silently, her tearful eyes fixed on the bird. Her hands felt stiff and lifeless after seeing its plight. But she could see that her husband and sons were doing their best for her parrot, doing it with great care too. They brought the cage inside and kept it there. Aditi didn't dare to touch the bird herself though she kept coming back to it looking at it with worried eyes. The bird appeared to be semi-conscious and did not move at all. Aditi's heart ached for her pet. Supratim laid his hand on her shoulder before going to the office.

"Don't worry," he told her softly, "Your bird is going to be alright."

What seemed really amazing was the fact that his prediction came to pass. The parrot got over its injury and started getting better. Whether it was due to Supratim's antiseptic cream, Aditi's earnest prayers, Papai and Tatai's care or its own life force, it was difficult to say. It got better and stronger with each coming day. The wound healed. The drugged air disappeared.

The bird would touch nothing the first few days except for the glucose water Tatai fed it with a dropper. On the third day it looked hungry and tried to eat the gram flour paste. Then it shook its battered wings by degrees and finally climbed up on its perch once more. A few more days found it screeching. A hoarse, tuneless croak but it sounded like music to Aditi's ears. It seemed a joyous announcement of its being alive.

Tatai had managed to locate the culprit the very next day. It was a flat-faced tomcat that ran wild in the neighbourhood. The tomcat had not escaped unscathed either. There was a big hole just under its eye made by the parrot's sharp beak. Tatai was determined to give the tomcat a good hiding.

Aditi had been too worried to get on with her writing. She spent a lot of time on the balcony looking out aimlessly. That was when she herself spotted the injured tomcat sitting quietly on the wall, an ugly wound under one eye. She felt sorry for the tomcat too. How could it possibly know that it was wrong to attack the bird? Cats and birds were natural enemies after all. It had only done what was inevitable. Aditi tried to explain it to her son.

"Don't hit the poor tomcat, Tatai. Leave it alone. How could it know that it's wrong to attack a bird?"

Supratim burst out laughing.

"Are you planning to treat the tomcat now? Should I get a

few more tubes of antiseptic cream from my office?" Things were smooth and normal between Aditi and Supratim once again. The wave of disharmony had disappeared into the sea of existence. That was life. Waves came and left traces of foam on the sand. The foam dried up and disappeared after a while leaving behind the wet sand on which people walked like before while the beach waited expectantly for new waves to arrive. Aditi was part of the same set up, after all. How could things be any different for her?

Life went on as usual. Aditi took up her writing once more. Hemen dropped in to take one of her stories. This time he was planning to send it to a bigger and better known magazine. Supratim went to Ranchi on tour for a couple of days. Tatai's summer vacation was on but it was difficult to catch sight of him as he was perpetually out. Papai was due to go off to Darjeeling with his friends for ten days some time the next week. Amidst all this Sujata dropped in unexpectedly one Sunday evening with her daughter. Supratim and Aditi spent a jolly evening with them, talking and joking all the time they were there. Sujata was mad when she heard about Aditi's writing.

"How mean of you to have kept it dark from me all this time," she roared, "Give me your stories right away. I'll return them safely after reading them."

Sujata's daughter was a great talker too, who out-talked even Tatai!

She was equally blunt with Aditi.

"How cruel of you to keep this poor bird captive, Aunty," she told Aditi.

Supratim was highly amused at her words. "Do you think the poor bird still remembers how to fly after remaining captive all this time? If you let it out it will flap a few steps and then fall flat on its face!"

The rains came down with a vengeance this year, although it was somewhat late to follow the torrid summer. The sky took on a permanent grey look with dark clouds hanging low. Rain came down hard and strong making up for its past delay by sheer quantity. The roads covered under sheets of water took on the look of Venice, except that there were no gondolas plying. The sun seemed like a missing planet, lost like the missing people advertised on the TV.

Aditi was ironing Supratim's half-dry shirt. Supratim's company was about to launch a new shampoo in the market. So a biggish party was being hosted the next evening, complete with fashion parade. Several well known models had been hired to show off their shampooed hair to the best advantage as they swayed their hips and tread along the catwalk. Supratim was particularly keen to wear this shirt to the party. The pressman who sat at the corner of their road had vanished with the sun.

The doorbell rang. Aditi opened the door and stared incredulously.

It was her brother come to visit her. On a rainy evening like this?

He held a dripping umbrella in one hand, a plastic wrapped packet on the other. His bulky leather portfolio was tucked under one arm.

"Are you surprised to see me?" asked Alakesh with an embarrassed smile.

Aditi had not been to their house in Amherst Street for a long time. The last time she had been there was more than a couple of months ago. Alakesh had not been home that day as he had been to look up an old friend.

Aditi felt happy to see her brother.

"Of course I am surprised. Who could have imagined that you might land up on such a rainy day?"

"What else could I do? I haven't had any news of you for ages since Tultuli's university is now closed for the summer."

Aditi spread out the dripping umbrella in front of the bathroom and got her brother a dry towel.

"Here, dry yourself first. You shouldn't have risked coming in such foul weather with your dislocated knee."

"My knee's fine. Nothing to worry about," said Alakesh handing her the plastic packet. "Let's gorge ourselves on potato chops and brinjal crisps like old times. Where are your boys?"

Alakesh did not come to her place very often but whenever he did he always brought something.

"They are hardly ever home in the evenings," said Aditi,

"Must be loitering about somewhere. Papai is due to leave for Darjeeling this Monday."

"Darjeeling in this rain! It's just the season for landslides and road blocks."

"That's what I told him too. But will he listen! Says Darjeeling has a distinct charm of its own during the rains."

"What kind of charm?"

"Goodness knows. They alone can tell! Wait a while and I'll get some tea. There is very little chance of my cook's landing up this evening."

Alakesh rubbed himself dry and dumped his bag on the centre table. Drying his hair carefully, he touched the sofa to see if his wet clothes had made it damp. He sat comfortably resting his head.

Aditi put the kettle on, deep in thoughts. Her brother rarely visited her without some good reason. Since he had braved such bad weather to come to her place the reason was likely to be an urgent one. He was looking quite a bit under the weather too.

"Have you come straight from the office?"

"Yes. Got out a little early as I wanted to see you."

"Then you must be hungry. Let me fry some luchis for you."

"No, no. Don't bother. Give me a little puffed rice if there's any."

Aditi was in a quandary. Neither of her sons touched puffed rice. Supratim took it once in a blue moon. So Aditi never bothered to stock any during the rainy season.

"Do let me make some", she insisted, " It's so long since you had lunch...."

"I suppose there isn't any puffed rice in the house? Never mind. Just make the tea and bring along the fried stuff. I have brought something else for you."

"What is it?"

"I'll show you. Get the tea first."

Aditi's heart thudded uncomfortably. These were the very words her brother used whenever he came to get anything signed by her. And he spoke in just this soft tone. Was it mother's National Saving Certificates this time? Had they matured already? Had Alakesh guessed that Supratim wouldn't be home this evening and had come to make the most of the opportunity? A sigh escaped from the bottom of her heart. She hated this bitter hide-and-seek game with her own brother. She arranged all the fried snacks on a large plate, made two big cups of tea and sat facing her brother.

"Show me what it is.'

"In a minute," said Alakesh pulling down the ends of his trousers. He had tucked them up when coming through the rain. "There's no water-logging in your locality, thanks be!"

"It's kind of the corporation to have raised the road this

side. But of course they did it because one of their councillors live right here."

"No wonder!"

"The road in front of your house must be under water today?"

Alakesh was silent for a moment.

"Haven't I asked you not to keep calling it my house, Khuku?"

Aditi bit into the crisp fried potato.

"Well, it is your house, isn't it?"

"No, it isn't. It belongs to us both, you and me."Alakesh drew a long breath. "One doesn't lose one rights to a place even if the papers say otherwise. I had got it transferred in my name because it makes it simpler to ask for a loan to get it repaired."

"Which you haven't done, now or ever," retorted Aditi. "Let's change the subject. What did you want to show me?"

Alakesh sat mute, at a loss for words. It was raining cats and dogs outside. He sat staring at the balcony, teacup in hand. The cage stood in the small passage next to the balcony. His eyes wandered there for a while. Then he put his cup on the table and picked up his bag. Pulling the zipper apart, he took out a thick brown paper parcel.

"What is it?" asked Aditi curiously.

"Open it and see."

Aditi's heart received a sudden jolt as she undid the parcel. It was crammed with notebooks. Her old notebooks where she had scribbled her stories during her school and college days. Under them lay some of her old school and college magazines.

"Where did you find these?" asked Aditi in an excited voice.

A faint smile lurked about Alakesh's lips as he replied, "I dug them out of mother's old black trunk since you have started writing again. Thought you might like to have them."

Aditi turned the pages with eager hands. Some of the pages held mere scribbles. Some had cartoon-like sketches with the names of friend written below. In some pages the same line was written over and over again. There were stories and poems the outline of a novel with a list of characters and what each was like. In another page she had simply written in huge letters, Aditi, you are a fool. You will never make it as a writer. One of the magazines contained her first published story, 'Mists'.

Aditi fingered the pages lovingly, touching the lines once penned by her. Were they mere letters or fragments of her life? Broken pieces of life, time and memories? The paper had turned yellow with time. The ink looked faded. And yet they seemed to call out to her, clearly! A hundred memories rushed in like waves, churning and swirling with the foam of her past while a little bird sang blithely within her heart.

"Are you happy to get them back, Khuku?" Alakesh asked softly.

Aditi lifted her eyes and looked steadfastly at her brother.

Not the brother of 53 summers but her 14-year-old brother who used to save up his tuck money to get her sweets. She saw herself licking them off the wrapping paper with great relish.

She nodded with the joy of a six-year-old.

"You came all this way in this rain just to bring me these?"

"At first I had thought I'd ask Tultuli to bring them over." Alakesh also seemed to walk back in time. "But I missed you. It's so long since I have given you anything you really care about with my own hands. All these years I have merely taken things from you."

Aditi felt tears prick at the back of her eyes.

"Uncle was telling me the other day that you are really writing well these days. And of course Tultuli is always singing your praises. I am a prosaic man myself and don't understand literature. But I feel proud to think that you are making a place for yourself there. You were regretting about losing time. I have brought back some of your lost moments. Pitch in now for all you're worth!"

Alakesh stood up, picked up his wet umbrella, and tucked his empty folio bag under his arms as he prepared to leave. Aditi stood at the door to see him off. As he walked down the steps Aditi wanted to call out to him as she would have done as a young girl. But now she felt a constriction at her throat as something seemed to stop her. Alakesh, her poor self-centred brother, was soon lost in the crowd below.

The rain had just stopped. A damp breeze swished across

the flat. Aditi's notebooks lay scattered on the centre table. Were they sheer notebooks or lost gems and pearls found miraculously? Had Alakesh ever taken anything from her that had been more valuable than these? Aditi walked up to the cage. Opening the door she touched the bird gently for the first time after it had been hurt. The wound was very nearly healed. Its body was beginning to look fresh and green once again. But it moved away in fear and jabbed at Aditi's hand. But the jab did not hurt her any more.

Chapter Eleven

The letterboxes belonging to Aditi's block hung in a row just below the staircase. Eight of them for eight different flats. The box marked Mazumdars was crammed with letters this morning. Two large covers for Supratim and Tatai. A letter from the insurance company, the electric bill and an inland letter from Supratim's brother in Lucknow. Aditi frowned over the electric bill that said Rs. 352. It had been Rs. 311 even last month. Forty-one rupees more this month! Aditi couldn't understand why. Their consumption of electricity remained virtually the same with nothing extra to justify this change. She looked at the sender's name of Papai's letter. It was marked Maryland University. He often received covers like these from abroad these days. There was one from the University of Arizona last month containing a thick prospectus. Papai had been livid because she had opened the letter.

"It's a very nasty habit to pry into the letters of other people, Mom", he had told her coldly.

Was Papai trying to go abroad? And therefore all the secrecy? But what was the harm in admitting it to others? Aditi laid the letter aside. Papai could open it himself after he returned from Darjeeling. There was no need to open Supratim's letter as she could guess who it was from. Some unknown Rajesh Gulati who kept sending some useless papers every now and then. Supratim did not know him from Adam nor had he any idea about how Gulati had managed to get hold of his address. His letters always contained share papers that were being released in the market every day by some company or the other. They reached Supratim too late nearly every time, after the last date for buying them was over. Supratim glanced at them and threw them into the wastepaper basket immediately. But sometimes if they arrived in time he read them carefully, calculating possible gains and losses before throwing them away. Supratim had his own agents in his office for buying or selling shares. But poor Rajesh Gulati did not know it. This letter sent by him would share the same fate as the others.

Aditi read his brother-in-law's letter as she climbed up the stairs. A simple, homely letter from Partha Pratim addressed to both of them, giving them the family news. Babai, their son, now in class vii, was getting serious about hockey and rushed around with his stick all day long. Kaveri, his wife, had suffered a heat stroke and had to be in bed for a whole week. She was better now after the advent of the monsoons. They were planning to come down to Calcutta for the pujas this year but it wouldn't be possible for them to stay for more than a week as Babai's vacation was a very short one this time. Both Partha and Kaveri had enquired how Aditi's writing was getting on. And there was the series of routine enquiries after Papai, Tatai, Aditi and Supratim's health.

Aditi smiled as she read through the letter. How strangely cool and insipid Partha had turned into over the years! And yet he had been her first and best friend at her in-laws' place when she was first married. Though her two sisters-in-law quite looked up to her these days, they had always considered her an arch enemy when she first arrived, behaving as though she had grabbed their goody goody elder brother unlawfully! They were almost childish in their resentment, keeping her away from Supratim until the wee hours of the morning, pretending to chat with her. They swiped all the perfumes and cosmetics Supratim brought for her. But Partha had never been like them. He was a friendly, happy-go-lucky and generous soul. He had got her a pretty sari with his self-earned money and always told her everything about his love affair with Kaveri. And now, over the years, Partha seemed like a total stranger while her sisters-in-law had become her friends. These were some of the incredible changes brought on by life.

Aditi stopped abruptly after reaching the third floor landing. A girl of twenty or thereabouts stood before their flat, pressing the doorbell. She wore a salwar suit, an orange chunni on her shoulder. She held a corner of the chunni, wrapping it round her finger as she looked tensely at the closed door of the next flat that belonged to Kalyani. Was she a salesgirl? But she wasn't carrying any goods. Aditi walked up fast and was soon beside her.

"Who do you want?"

The girl looked startled. "Does Sayantan Majumdar live here?"

"Yes, he does," said Aditi smiling, "I am his mother."

"I see," said the girl looking uncomfortable, "Is he at home?"

"No, he isn't. He is in Darjeeling."

"Is he?" The girl sounded surprised, "When will he return?"

"He is due to start from New Jalpaiguri tomorrow and reach here the day after."

"I see."

"Would you like to leave a message for him?"

"No, no," the girl shook her head nervously, "I shall contact him myself after he returns."

Aditi felt curious. Why did she look so nervous? Her voice sounded familiar too. She was climbing down the stairs slowly.

"Just a moment," Aditi called after her, "You didn't tell me your name."

"My name? There's no need to tell Sayantan anything about me."

Aditi looked bewildered. "But I'd like to know your name. What is it?"

"Sreya."

Aditi tried to remember the names of Papai's classmates. She knew the names of some of the girls. Chandana, Sutanuka, Baishakhi and some others had come to her place to meet him. Was Sreya one of them too? She looked at her curiously.

"Are you one of Sayantan's classmates?"

"No."

"What is your subject?"

"I am a student of English Honours."

"In the same college?"

"No, I am from Jadavpur."

"Where do you live?"

"At Beleghata."

Suddenly Aditi put two and two together. It must be the girl who called up Papai every night.

She tried to stop her.

"You can't get back all that distance right away," she told her, "Stop for a while."

"I haven't come from Beleghata, Aunty. I had gone to college. But our class was cancelled at the last moment. So I thought I'd drop by and look up Sayantan."

"Never mind the reason for your coming. Sayantan will be mad with me if he hears that a friend of his had come to look him up and had gone back right from the door without so much as a cup of tea. Come in."

Aditi opened the lock of their door. Sreya stood on the landing looking uncertain. Aditi looked at her with the scrutinizing eyes of a detective. The girl was remarkably pretty with big, expressive eyes, short, wavy hair and a fair skin. But she was blushing with confusion at the moment and also perspiring profusely.

"Come in," said Aditi in a commanding voice.

The monsoon seemed to be taking a break after a few days' non-stop rain. The sky was covered with heavy clouds through which the sun peeped out at intervals. Hesitant sunbeams drew pictures in water colour on the dark blue sky. The same magic play of light and shade entered Aditi's living room.

Sreya sat in a corner of the sofa looking about her with the scared eyes of a rabbit, wiping her face every now and then with her chunni.

Aditi brought her a glass of cold orange squash and sat facing her.

"Sayantan is a student of St. Xaviers, not Jadavpur. Where did you meet him?"

"At their annual college festival."

"I see. So you haven't known him for very long, have you?"

"No. Just about seven or eight months."

"Wait a minute," said Aditi pretending to think, "Aren't you the girl who calls him up every night? And you always disconnect the line whenever Sayantan's Dad takes the call?"

Sreya had been sipping the cold drink slowly. She started at the words, choked and began to cough, her face a fiery red.

Aditi wanted to laugh at her confusion. She just smiled and said, "He was on the line talking to you for hours even the night before he left. Didn't he tell you then that he was going to Darjeeling?"

Sreya sat silent for a while. Then she looked straight at Aditi and said, "I haven't called him up of late, Aunty."

"Then who was he talking to? I am sure it's your voice I heard when giving him the phone."

"Believe me, Aunty, I haven't been in touch with him for over two months."

"Why?"

Sreya sat with downcast eyes and did not answer.

When a mother is too naive there are many obvious things that she fails to notice. But if she is too possessive she manages to see more than what actually exists. Aditi continued to smile as she asked, "What did you two quarrel about?"

Sreya sat silent.

"Funny that you should feel so shy to talk about it when you've come all this way to find him."

Still Sreya did not respond.

"When did you see him last?"

"Sometime in April, on the 25th of Baisakh."

"Where?"

"We had been to a movie together."

"Which movie was it?"

Sreya did not reply.

Aditi stopped asking questions. She had heard quite enough, anyway. Perhaps they had had a serious disagreement. Papai had a strange streak of obstinacy in him which he didn't express the same way that Tatai did. Tatai blew hot and cold but it was easy to understand him. Papai kept his resentments buried deep within. Once Aditi had asked him not to eat ice creams after he had a bad throat. Papai had pleaded a few times and then held his tongue. But he absolutely refused to touch ice cream after that for months altogether though both Aditi and Supratim begged him to. He made no scenes, just refused to touch it. Firmly and with a smiling face. Perhaps he was facing something of the same sort with Sreya.

Aditi gave her a cool look and said, "I won't ask you what you quarrelled about if you don't want to tell me, but ...."

"There was no quarrel or disagreement between us, Aunty," said Sreya in a clear and steady voice.

"Then what went wrong?"

"I really don't know. He has been avoiding me steadily without any reason since that evening. If I ask him to meet me he makes excuses. If I call him up, he doesn't answer."

Though Sreya tried to speak normally Aditi heard the catch in her voice. She didn't know what to make of the whole episode even after Sreya left. Was Papai being unkind to her for no rhyme or reason? He must have been badly hurt by something in her behaviour. He had always been an introvert. Perhaps that's why he preferred to avoid her quietly without getting into arguments about it.

Aditi couldn't put her mind to work that whole afternoon and simply made scratches with her pen without writing a word. She just couldn't put Sreya's downcast face out of her mind. What sort of a girl was she? From her looks and manners she appeared to belong to a good family. But an innocent face didn't necessarily mean an innocent heart. Rina, her younger sister-in-law had gone to meet her boyfriend even on the morning of her engagement with another man and had not bothered to let her boyfriend know even then that she was getting married to someone else. It was Ajoy, her boyfriend, who had told Aditi about the whole episode years later. Could anyone have guessed from Rina's overjoyed looks on her wedding day that she had been going steady with Ajoy for well over a year? So it was not really possible for Aditi to guess from Sreya's gloomy face what had actually happened to them both. Or with whom Papai had been speaking that night in a low voice, a smiling face and intent looks.

It was dusk by the time Supratim returned home. He had been looking unusually worried the last few days. But this evening his face spelt disaster. Aditi knew what he was worried about. Jameson India was about to merge with Lotus India where Supratim worked. Everyone in his office was worried not knowing just what turn things might take. But why did he look so very upset today? Had things come to a head?

Supratim rushed in to have a bath, switched on the TV and picked up a bottle. Aditi came and sat next to him. She knew he would be annoyed if she asked him anything.

"May I tell you something?" she asked in a timid voice.

Supratim stared at the TV screen though he saw nothing.

"What is it?" He asked, without moving his eyes from the screen.

"Let's go for a movie tonight. A late night show."

Supratim gave her a cold look. "Why?"

"Because we haven't been to one for ages."

Supratim continued to sip his drink. "Do you feel this is a time for a celebration?"

Aditi wanted to annoy him. Perhaps anger would prompt him to open his mouth and tell her what was bothering him.

"So it seems, from the way you have been drinking right from the moment you landed up."

"Have you any objection to my drinking?"

"Of course I have. Have you forgotten that your BP was 140 by 95, the last time you got it checked?"

"Could be. I have other things to think of besides my BP."

His voice was spiritless. Aditi remained silent for a while. Then she said, "Why drink on an empty stomach? You know it never agrees with you. Shall I ask Tatai to get you some savouries, mixed gram or potato crisps?"

"No thanks."

"You know you will suffer from acidity if you don't eat something with your drink. Then you will complain of a burning chest all night."

"I'll sleep on the sofa so as not to disturb you at night."

This time it was Aditi who was mad. She had thought of telling him about Sreya's visit. But it went totally out of her mind after seeing Supratim's face.

"What on earth has happened to make you look like a barn owl?" asked Aditi.

Her temper made him speak his mind where softness and pleading had failed.

"It has happened finally" he said in a glum voice.

"What has?"

"The merging, of course. Both Board Members sat for a joint meeting at Mumbai this evening. The final decision has just come through."

"So what? You have told me often enough that it is not going to affect your job."

"You must be crazy! Don't you know that I feel like committing suicide this evening?"

"Good heavens! Why?" Aditi cried.

"Mr Gilani has gone."

"Is he dead? How did it happen? Stroke?"

"Don't talk rubbish. Why should he die? He has resigned. You don't know how fond he was of me, Phool. I was like a son to him."

Aditi realised that Supratim was already high when she heard him addressing her by the forgotten, much-loved name. She merely said, "How could he possibly be like a father to you? You both are practically of the same age!"

"Oh well, it's just a way of expressing how I feel! Age has nothing to do with fatherhood. He always looked after me and stood by me like a father. Do you understand?"

"Yes I do," she said taking the bottle away from him. "You are going to work and do your best for the company. How does it matter who the boss is?"

Supratim gave Aditi a hurt, stricken look.

"Get up," said Aditi. "Come and have dinner. I'll call Tatai. Now, don't speak all this rot before him."

Tatai took the whole situation in the moment he saw the state his father was in and smiled to himself. Aditi frowned at him and laid a finger on her lips to stop him from making any comments.

The next evening Supratim was in a completely different mood when he returned from office. He shouted, threw his arms about and yelled blue murder because one Vivek Ahuja was coming in as the big boss of the entire eastern region replacing Gilani. He was a mere lad of thirty-two and Supratim would have to work directly under him. What seemed the unkindest cut of all was the fact that Vivek Ahuja didn't belong to Lotus India at all. He was the nephew of the existing chairman of Jameson India. It was too much to take! Supratim would resign and find a job elsewhere. There were many other companies who'd be only too glad to take him.

Papai returned to Calcutta amidst all this confusion. The train had been over four hours late. There had been no light and no water in their compartment most of the time. A dog-tired Papai slept like a log all day.

One tends to forget the most obvious of things if one is worried. Aditi, worried sick about her husband, didn't remember about Sreya's visit even after Papai returned. In their married life of 23 odd years Aditi had often seen Supratim worried. But it was nothing like his present state of mind. He had always been a practical man with his feet on solid ground and Aditi always had full faith in him. But what if he did something really crazy in his present mood? Lotus India was his whole life. He often teased Aditi by saying 'this company runs in my veins'! Would it be easy for the same man, now fifty plus, to find a job elsewhere? And would it make him happy even if he did?

Aditi remembered about Sreya a couple of days later. Papai had been out all morning, returning home well after two and immediately sat down with a sheaf of papers. Aditi came to his room.

"What's up? Have you seen what time it is? What about

your bath and lunch?"

Papai was filling up a form carefully. He looked up and said, "I know. But I must run to the post office first."

"In this blazing heat? And you've just come in! Why couldn't you go to the post office before coming home if it's that urgent?"

Papai laughed at his mother's childish question.

"I'd have done it if it had been possible. Do get me glass of cold orange squash."

"Are you trying for a job?"

"No."

"Then what are all these applications for?"

"You'll get to know in good time."

"Are you planning to sit for the GRE? Do you want to go to the States for higher studies?"

Papai looked at his mother through the corner of his eyes. "A good guess," he said.

"But why do you need to go abroad? What's wrong with completing your studies here?"

"Please, Mom, I haven't gone abroad as yet. I'm merely sending in an application."

Papai closed his pen. "Please get me a cold drink. I'm dying of thirst."

Aditi suddenly remembered Sreya as she took out the bottle of orange squash from the fridge. Was it because she had used it the last time when preparing a cold drink for Sreya?

She took him the glass of squash and asked, "What's the name of the girl who calls you up every night?"

"Why do you ask?"

"No particular reason."

"Then?"

"She isn't one of your classmates, is she?"

"I must say you are getting to be jolly good at guessing."

Papai kept his empty glass down and turned to his application once again.

Aditi couldn't decide what to ask him next. Would it right to tell him about Sreya's visit without finding out how close they actually were? After all, Papai was a grown up now. Would he mind her questioning him too closely?

"Do you know Sreya?" she asked in a hesitant voice.

Papai was visibly startled. He stopped writing. "Sreya who?"

"You should know that better than me."

"I don't know any Sreya." Papai turned away his face. "How did you chance upon the name? Did someone called Sreya ring up while I was away?"

No, she came here herself, Aditi was about to say but stopped herself in time. Was there something really wrong between the two?

"It's difficult to keep secrets from one's mother," she said lightly. "I can plainly see from your face that...."

"Stop it, mother," shouted Papai, turning his head with a jerk. A strange smiled lurked about his lips. "I don't know who has been telling you tales but take it from me, I never had any relationship with anyone called Sreya. Nor do I have one at present."

"Do you mean to say you don't know Sreya?"

"Of course I know her. Or rather, knew her. She's a cheap sort. Had been after me good and strong. But I've no use for her kind."

Aditi was somewhat surprised to see Papai's face completely bereft of feelings as he said it.

"Isn't Sreya the girl you spoke with every day, for hours?"

"No, she isn't."

"Then who is the girl?"

"Why are you so curious about my personal affairs?"

"Shouldn't a mother be curious about her own son's life?"

"Yes. But only to the extent he chooses to disclose and not beyond. Now, please leave me alone. I've a lot of work to do."

Aditi went out of the room, a hurt look on her face. The smoke within her heart was getting thicker by the minute. Was Papai lying to her? Or was it Sreya who had lied? And why did either of them have to lie to her at all? She wasn't an old fogey, unable to understand how young people felt. There was no need for Papai to hide things from her. Was Sreya really the cheap kind, bent on chasing her son? Had she come to give her a false impression about him? But how could that be? She hadn't tried to speak to Aditi at all. It was she who had made her come in and asked her questions. Should she have told Papai about her visit? The thought haunted Aditi but she could find no solution that seemed satisfactory. She was worried enough about Supratim. Now Papai was causing her fresh worry. With both these on her mind she was in no mood to turn to her writing. She tried to complete a story for two whole days without any success. Things continued to remain dark and uncertain, so far as her husband sons and, perhaps, she herself was concerned.

Chapter Twelve

Anxiety has a life of its own. Like living creatures it expresses itself in many ways. Sometimes it glimmers like a slow burning fire within. At other times it appears on the mind's sky like flakes of clouds, covering it up completely as it extends further and further. Or it might take the form of air and bloat up one's existence, like an oversize balloon. Supratim's anxiety about his office belonged to the last kind. His worries always took on the form of balloons, no matter what size they were, and burst like one when they ended. He almost floated into the house a few evenings later. He seemed to tread on air as he clutched several big boxes containing cakes, pastries and patties from one of the best known shops on Park Street. He was literally bubbling with excitement as he called out to his sons who happened to be home that evening.

"Papai! Tatai! Come here, quick. Tuck in while they're still hot and fresh!"

Aditi looked at him in wide eyed wonder. Had he won a

lottery? Or had the pressure of anxiety driven him nuts?

"What's wrong with you? And how can we possibly tuck in such a mountain of goodies? I doubt if even the 100 sons of Dhritarashtra would be able finish the lot !"

Supratim ignored her and broke into a song – *dil hai ki maanta nahin* ..

"Please, Dad, that song requires a totally different kind of situation," said Tatai biting into a Black Forest pastry.

"What kind of situation?"

"Oh well, not quite a family situation like this. You'd require ... let me see.... yes, a dim blue light and you'd have to be at least 25 years younger, your waist a great deal trimmer and Mom would have to be ..."

"Shut up!" said Aditi laughing, "You wicked boy, how dare you joke about your parents!"

"Let him alone," said Supratim joining in the laughter, "Don't you remember what Chanakya says about fathers and sons once a son crosses the age of sixteen .... what's it, something about treating him like a friend? I can't remember the words of the sloka. Papai, don't you remember it?"

Papai was busy devouring a chicken patty and replied, "We didn't have Sanskrit in our school, Dad."

"Really? Now, that's strange! It used to be compulsory when we were in school. Ah, such a beautiful language! So musical! Anyway, I'm sure you can guess which sloka I am talking about."

"Yes, I can but I can't guess what the celebration is all about" remarked Aditi.

"There is a good reason," said Supratim, "But all in good time!"

Supratim went inside to change his office clothes and wash his face and hands. When he returned to the drawing room he made himself comfortable on the sofa. Putting his feet up on the centre table he lit a cigarette.

"My assessment of the office situation was quite wrong."

"Nothing new about that," said Aditi.

"What I mean is, I was about to commit a great blunder. Had I handed in my papers in the heat of the moment it would have been the biggest mistake of my life."

Aditi heaved a sigh of relief. The anxiety had not been a in the nature of a cloud this time. The balloon of depression had burst already. She gave him a saucy look. "I hope you don't require the bottle for celebrating tonight?"

"Goodness, no! Do you take me for a drunkard? Make me a super duper cup of coffee instead."

Sabita had already left after cooking dinner. Aditi made two cups of milky coffee for her sons and proper strong coffee for herself and Supratim. She went to sit beside him, cup in hand. Supratim did not keep them in suspense much longer. He announced with an air of importance that the company had decided to give him a full time car. He was also going to have several additional perks in future along with a thumping big salary hike. Supratim didn't spell out the exact amount before his sons but added that he'd have to go to Mumbai the next week. The new manager had called a meeting with the area managers of every department.

Aditi particularly enjoyed Supratim's dramatic way of making a happy announcement. She felt equally delighted with his unexpected piece of good luck. As delighted as Supratim expected her to be.

Papai had already gone out. Tatai was listening to music in his own room. Aditi and Supratim sat talking in the drawing room.

"I didn't really expect you to get quite so many perks," said Aditi laughing happily.

"What did you expect?"

"Seeing you look so overjoyed I thought your Gilani had returned to your company."

"Him! He's a cheat of the first water! A sneak thief, if you ask me. You have no idea how much of the company's money he had already swiped. It was Vivek Ahuja who caught him at it. The company is seriously considering bringing a criminal charge against him."

Aditi was at a loss for words!

"Weren't you the one who called him an angel, a father figure and what not?"

"All that's in the past. Gilani is just a nightmare now."

"So your Vivek Ahuja is a good man?"

"Good? He is a gem of a man! I had no idea that he had done his MBA from Harvard. His knowledge and concept about marketing is simply amazing. And yet, he is such a modest, unassuming person!"

"What happened to Gilani? Did he do the vanishing trick with all his ill-gotten gains?"

"You're quite impossible! Don't you know that people who are so high up don't hide like petty sneak thieves? On the contrary they strut around like peacocks. If you must know, he has joined Peterson & Peterson."

"And they took him despite his record?"

"Oh well, cheating isn't considered a crime when you are that high up. It's regarded as an extra-curricular activity, like Papai's hockey, Tatai's swimming and your writing."

Supratim guffawed at his own ability to find just the right comparisons. Then he said with a note of regret, "It's I who remained an honest fool all my life. I never could go for any unlawful gains at the cost of my company."

Aditi frowned at his words. "Why not? What prevented you?"

"It's not due to any fault of my own. It's because that old man – your father-in-law – brainwashed me with all kinds of stupid ideals. 'Remain honest! Never try to fill up your pockets with ill-gotten gains! You'll see that you will be able to manage fine if only you stick to the right path.' And I suppose I have managed to do it, haven't I?"

Aditi had never imagined his father-in-law to be a die hard idealist. On the contrary he had always seemed to be a timid, peace-loving man. He held a middling kind of post in an aluminium factory. He loved to read books and was fond of classical music, often attending concerts until the wee hours of the morning. He never interfered with anybody. Aditi felt happy to think that such an unassuming man had actually brainwashed his son with a degree of idealism. But was it a positive virtue of doing good actively or the negative virtue of not doing wrong? How did deliberate wrong-doers face their wives? Aditi couldn't have done it herself!

"Since you have managed things quite well so far sticking to the right path why regret the fact that you couldn't do otherwise?" she asked Supratim.

"Because I keep seeing the others all around me ... doing it all the time!"

A sudden thought struck Aditi.

"Did you know that your Gilani was a cheat?"

"The whole world knew it," said Supratim unthinkingly and stopped himself from saying any more. "Why ask a lot of stupid questions? Don't ruin my good mood."

Aditi held her tongue. But she went rigid for a moment. An unforeseen shadow threatened to ruin the happy evening.

For a second Supratim seemed to be someone else. An amoral, backboneless, empty-headed worshipper of people who had made it big by their obvious dishonesty. But only just for a second. Aditi blamed herself for thinking the worst of a man she had lived with comfortably for 23 long years.

Supratim switched on the TV. He surfed aimlessly for a while and finally found the film channel. He settled down to watch the film. Stretching his arm across Aditi's shoulders he asked, "What's the menu for tonight's dinner?"

"Rice with Ileesh-fish curry." Aditi drew away from his touch.

"No mangoes?"

"Yes, there are. I'll cut them at the time of dinner."

"I'd like to dine early tonight. I really need a night of peaceful sleep. Get me the newspaper and my glasses, will you?"

Aditi gave him what he wanted and came to the balcony to fetch the cage indoors. The parrot was fast asleep. It looked up for a second when Aditi touched the cage and went back to sleep. It could recognise Aditi's scent even when asleep. But her presence did not disturb the bird. It continued to sleep peacefully.

There was a small group of people in front of the gate, with three or four boys shouting something. The flickering street lights hurt the eyes. There were no stars above. The sky wore a reddish look. A gentle breeze was blowing, so lightly that one could hardly feel it. Was it going to pour again tonight?

Figures moved across the TV screen as Supratim marked the newspaper in pencil. Strains of western music wafted out from the boys' room. The whole scene appeared somewhat unreal to Aditi. Supratim was tapping on the centre table with his pencil to the beat of the music. His head moved in rhythm with the song being picturised on the screen, and sometimes to the beat of the Western music. Did Supratim have any rhythm of his own? Aditi turned her head away in distaste.

Tultuli dropped by the next evening on her way back from the university. Aditi was trying to complete her story for the second time after sending off Malina's mother. Tultuli peeped inside the bedroom, saw her working and stuck out her tongue in embarrassment.

"You were writing! I shouldn't have disturbed you at this time."

Papers were strewn all across the floor. Three pillows were scattered in different directions, papers tucked under them. Papers were pressed down under the ash-tray and the powder box too. A thick Bengali dictionary lay open.

But though Tultuli's arrival meant interrupted work Aditi didn't mind it in the least. Tultuli was always welcome in her house no matter when she chose to come. Somehow her arrival always filled her heart with a feeling of pure joy. Was it because she carried with her the fragrance of Aditi's lost childhood and home? Perhaps!

"Never mind my writing. It hardly matters if I stop for a

while. My efforts are like a blind man trying to do embroidery. It's nothing more than a pastime, really."

"I don't care what you call it, Pishi, but writing is a serious hobby. Now that you have four stories published you are a full-fledged author."

Aditi's heart gave a joyful bound.

No matter what her own family thought of her writing, her niece at least took it seriously and thought of her as a writer. So did her brother though he had not read any of her stories.

"You have come after a long time," she told Tultuli.

"It's difficult to come all this way unless the university is open."

"When did it reopen?"

"Last week. I had been planning to come ever since but it has been raining so much of late that I didn't dare to take a chance. But Baba was very angry with me for not looking you up so I made up my mind to brave it today, come hail or high water."

Aditi seemed to catch a glimpse of her brother's face for a moment. The way he had looked at her the last time, going away quietly with tired steps leaving her gloating with her old notebooks.

"I'll give you my stories this evening. Take them for your father. When he was here the last time it was raining so hard that I didn't remember to give them to him then."

"Did Baba come here? When was it?"

"About a fortnight back. Didn't he tell you about it?"

"No, he didn't."

Aditi dropped the subject. Putting away her scattered papers she asked Tultuli to sit down. There were loads of cakes and pastries in the fridge. Aditi brought a couple of them for Tultuli. A vague question that had been tormenting her all morning suddenly came into sharp focus the moment she saw Tultuli. Aditi could no longer keep it to herself.

"Can you get me a piece of information?" she asked her.

"About what?"

"A girl who is also a student in your university. A student of English honours."

"What's her name? And what year is she in?"

"I don't know the year. I don't know her full name either. Her name is Sreya."

Tultuli stopped abruptly, spoon in hand. She gave Aditi a straight look.

"What do you want to know?"

"Do you know the girl?"

"What exactly do you want to know about her?"

"Nothing in particular. Just what kind of a girl she is."

"Why?"

Tultuli's sharp and direct look made her feel uneasy. She also felt disturbed for no apparent reason. Papai was a gem of a boy. How could she distrust what he had told her about the girl? And yet ... she couldn't drive away her doubts.....

Aditi decided to make a clean breast of the whole episode to Tultuli, right from Sreya's arrival, what she had told her and what Papai had said about her. Tultuli sat still for a while not speaking a single word. The fan whirled overhead. A light shower started outside. But despite it the heat seemed to burn into one's skin. The light outside grew dim all of a sudden. The whistle of an electric train tore the silence of the air. Tultuli finished the pastries in silence and left the empty plate in the kitchen sink. Then she wiped her face with a corner of her off-white chunni.

"I know the girl you are talking about, Pishi, she said in a low voice. I didn't know her at first, not until I saw Papai going around with her all over the campus. Then I went and spoke to her myself. Sreya is a really nice girl, Pishi. Good at her studies, well behaved and has a soft, quiet temperament."

It sounded just what Aditi had feared.

Perhaps they both quarrelled over something and now neither of them was willing to make it up.

Tultuli sat down on the bed. She looked hesitant for a while and then blurted out, "Papai isn't quite like what he appears to be. Even I used to think that he only cared about academics and had no time for anything else, least of all girls." She took a deep breath. "Papai is my own cousin and I hate talking against him. But Sreya isn't the only girl he has been going around with. There are two or three more with whom he shares the same kind of relationship. ... at one and the same time."

Aditi looked at her, disbelief in her face.

"How do you know that?"

"I do know it for a fact. And I have also heard about it from Sreya. Ask Papai if he hasn't been going around with a girl named Nandini and another called Devanjali. There is yet another who lives somewhere near the Gol Park. I don't know her name. She isn't from our university. Sreya had met me recently and was in tears about the whole episode. She is dead serious about Papai. I thought I'd speak to Papai about her myself. I didn't know that she had already come to your place looking for him. But you know, Pishi, it isn't decent of Papai to play around with so many girls like this."

Tultuli's words did not seem like words to Aditi. They were a series of invisible slaps across her face. Was this the same Papai who would refuse to eat unless Aditi fed him with her own hands? The same Papai who went to sleep clutching a corner of her sari after her brother was born because with Tatai in her lap there was now no room for him? Had this same Papai now turned into such an expert playboy? Aditi had always been so proud of her sons, telling herself that she had brought them up to be not just brilliant in academics, but also boys with strong characters, steady, honest and dependable. But was this the actual reality?

Aditi folded up her seething rage like a crumpled piece of

paper within her heart. But she let it out at dinner time in the presence of everyone, deliberately and cleverly.

Papai was eating steadily, a thriller open before him. Tatai had his eyes glued to the TV where a horror movie was being telecast. Supratim sat scrutinizing his plate of salad with a happy, contented expression.

Aditi served fresh chapatis all round and asked Papai in a cold voice, "Papai, have you told your father that you are planning to sit for your GRE?"

"Yes, I have." Papai did not move his eyes from the pages of his book.

"So, it was meant to be a secret from me alone, isn't it?"

"I had to tell Dad. After all, he's the one who is going to shell out the examination fees."

"How much is it?"

"Around three thousand."

"Supposing you get through, what do you plan to do next?"

"Go abroad for higher studies."

"Why? Can't you do your masters and Ph. D from here?"

"Of course I can. But what's the use?"

"What do you mean?"

"The scope for research is very limited here. In the universities abroad you not only have a fantastic lab, wonderful journals and wonderful guides... it's a different world altogether. Sitting here you can't even imagine the size of the libraries those universities have and the kind of facilities available there."

"But it's this country that has developed your brains and your ability to work."

Papai put his book away and looked at Aditi.

"Sorry, I can't understand what you are getting at."

Aditi looked back. "Why? Is it so very difficult? I admit that everything is just wonderful out there. But then why do such places require a base that is the product of a university belonging to a useless and worthless country like ours?"

Papai shrugged. "I guess because I have been unfortunate enough to be born here, what else?"

Supratim was listening to the dialogue between mother and son with an amused face. He smiled to himself.

"Do you intend to return to the land of your birth after your studies are complete?"

"Aren't you going rather fast? Let me get the chance of going abroad first."

"Supposing you do? What will you do then?"

"It's a hypothetical question, Mom."

"But you must have given it some thought."

"What do you feel? Should I return?"

"Forget about me. Tell me what you feel."

Papai thought for a few moments and said, "Tell me, what I would gain by coming back here? If I get the chance of some wonderful research out there....? There's very little chance of my finding it in my own country. I am keen on astro-physics. Space study. What scope do I have of studying it here? Forget about the NASA. Do we have even a decent observatory in India?"

Papai looked at his father and brother.

"Coming back here would either mean teaching in the university or tinkering about with some outdated, outmoded, archaic instruments without any serious gain."

Tatai burst out laughing. "Aren't you keeping your main reason for going abroad under your hat? Why don't you admit straight out that you'll also make tons of money out there and live like a king?"

"Yes, that too, of course. Life is far easier abroad. No crowds, hawkers, slums or pollution to speak of. Who doesn't crave for a calm and quiet life?"

"But I prefer to live in my own country," said Tatai, "Dirty, congested and overcrowded as it is. I'll manage to make all the money I want to right here. There's so much money flying around... hundreds and thousands and millions .... If you only know how to grab it. I know I shall manage to do it somehow."

Aditi looked at both. "So your only aim in life is to make money, isn't that so?"

Supratim decided to put in a word. Giving his sons an indulgent look he said, "That's what all sharp and intelligent people aim at these days. There's no reason why my boys won't succeed just because I have never managed to make much money."

Aditi felt that she belonged to a different planet altogether. Quite different from the rest of her family. She had tried to do so much for her sons, spent so much of her time on them and was this the net result? A huge naught!

She looked at Papai. "Then don't pretend that you are going for the sake of study and research. Admit that you are just going there to buy prosperity." Her voice was dry and bereft of emotion.

Supratim was about to answer back but Papai stopped him. He gave Aditi a straight look and asked, "Do you think prosperity can be bought for nothing? Unless my research is worth something to them why will they give me my prosperity – house, car and all the rest of it? You don't expect them to give it for nothing, just by looking at my face?"

"You are going to spend your life serving another country. Of what advantage will it be to us?"

"Science has no country, Mom. Has Newton's country been the only one to profit from his discovery?"

"Newton was not born in a poor country like ours. And he didn't sell his brains to another country simply because it was a richer country."

Papai smiled. "If I am really lucky enough to sell my brains some day, you will have a share of my gains, Mom. In dollars!"

She might have reacted differently to his words some other time. But Aditi was determined to expose Papai tonight.

"Very well. Perhaps your old parents will be happy with your dollars. But what about yourself? Won't you miss us at all if you settle down abroad?"

Supratim was annoyed.

"Why are you after my elder son tonight? The poor boy has been going all out, trying to ensure a bright future. Instead of encouraging him to do his best you are ..."

"Well, I have not discouraged him either. I am not clever like you people and my understanding is limited. I merely wanted to know how people like our charwoman are going to benefit from Papai's sending out rockets in NASA. Since Papai has done his basic studies here, even Malina's mother has made some contribution to his studies. Hasn't she, Tatai? What does your economic theory say?"

Tatai was delighted to find his brother in a quandary.

"Yes, the state does subsidise higher education to a large extent. Which means even Malina's mother contributes to it."

"Forget Malina's mother," said Aditi, "What I want to ask you Papai, is, won't you miss us at all out there?"

Papai's toleration had crossed its limits.

"You are really going too far with your hypothetical assessments. Since you understand so much you should also realise that the world is getting to be a global village day by day. You will be at one end and I shall be at another. Of course there will be journeys to and fro. But sticking to one's country for life just because one's parents live here is a medieval sentiment, out of place in today's world. Do you really feel that your sons should sacrifice their career, their future, and all hopes of making it good, simply to look after you when you are old? Do you consider it sane thinking?"

Aditi could see the real Papai at long last. The mask was down. A cold and heartless robot stood before her. She wanted to probe further and see how much more it could take.

"You tell me what is sane? Is it sane to play around with one girl after another just because you are planning to run away from here? Is it sane to throw a good, sensitive girl into the dustbin the moment you are tired of her and end the matter by branding her a cheap female?"

The place seemed to be struck by a sudden lightning. Papai stood still like a rock. Tatai looked curiously from one face to the other. The mango seed slipped from Supratim's hand and fell on the floor.

Aditi gave Papai another sharp look.

"Why are you silent? Tell me what you call the relationship that exists between you and all those girls, Devanjali, Nandini, Sreya and the girl from Gol Park."

"Mother, you are crossing limits," growled Papai standing up.

"Who has been crossing limits, you or me? Tell me, am I wrong? Haven't you been behaving like a rotten playboy with all these girls?"

"If I am, it's my personal business, not yours. Why are you butting in into my private life?"

"Because I happen to be your mother."

"So what? That doesn't give you the right to intrude or interfere with my life."

Aditi was too angry to speak. Tears streamed down her cheeks as she sat with her head bent.

Papai tramped out of the place and shut himself in his own room. Tatai also left the table soon after.

Supratim sat speechless looking disturbed.

It was raining heavily outside. The balcony was flooded. The parrot moved within the cage restlessly. Supratim forgot to wash his hands.

"You shouldn't have said all that," he told Aditi in a whisper.

Aditi looked at him in surprise.

"Why don't you realise the fact that the boys are grown up now?" said Supratim, "They have a life of their own. So they are not likely to put up with our interference where their own world is concerned."

Aditi blew her nose.

"Do you mean to tell me that you support Papai's actions?"

"It's not a question of supporting or not supporting. They are grown up now. Let them live their own life. It is not right to pull them up like this."

"Even when they do something wrong?"

"Yes, even then. Let them learn things the hard way. Didn't you tell me the other day that one shouldn't interfere in the personal lives of others?"

"I had said it in a totally different context, when speaking of Deepak and Sharmila. Divorce is a very personal affair."

"This is a private affair too. Deepak and Sharmila are adults. So is your son. So are the girls he is supposed to be involved with. It's wrong to intrude into the private life of others. Let him sort it out himself. Who are you to come between? And if any of these girls come bleating to you, just throw them out. Why don't you stick to writing stories instead of trying to play god in the lives of others? I feel for my brilliant son! Really, Aditi you were very wrong to have spoken to him as you did!"

The rain storm grew stronger by the minute. Streaks of lightning cut across the dark sky. Large drops of rain lashed upon the world. Aditi was crying. For whom were the tears? Aditi wasn't sure!

Chapter Thirteen

"Aditi, where are you? Quick, go and fetch some sweets!"

Hemen called out the moment he stepped into the flat. Ranjan followed close behind.

"Not just sweets. You must stand us a proper lunch," he said in a voice full of suppressed thrill.

The sofa was heaped with new coloured curtains. Aditi had been putting them up with Tatai's help. She put up new curtains during the pujas every year without fail. But this year there was some unexpected delay in getting them stitched and they arrived well after Diwali. Aditi picked up the curtains from the sofa and dumped them in her bedroom hurriedly.

"I understand that I owe you people a feed but I have no idea what the reason might be. Is there a special reason?" Aditi asked.

"Haven't you seen the advertisement in today's paper?"

"What advertisement?"

"Oh sorry. I had forgotten that you get the Bengali newspaper only on Sundays."

"What's it all about, Hemen Mama? Please don't be so mysterious!"

Before Hemen could reply Ranjan said, "The advertisement in today's paper carries your name. Your story is scheduled to appear in tomorrow's Sunday supplement."

Aditi's heart gave a sudden bound of joy. The blood rushed madly in her veins. Could it really be true? But she took care not to show how excited she actually felt so that the others might not think her childish.

"It's all thanks to Hemen Mama," she said in a grateful voice.

"Why? Because I collected the story from you? I merely played the courier, nothing more."

" But if you hadn't taken it from me ..... You know so many people ....."

"Really, Aditi, you are the limit! Your story got selected on its own merit. I had absolutely no hand in it. Don't allow yourself to develop an inferionity complex about your own work. It isn't healthy."

"I knew how talented you are the moment I read your first story," said Ranjan. "Now you merely need the time to concentrate and hone your talent further."

Tatai sat on the sofa listening to their talk. The magic autumn evening had been beckoning him for a long time and he had been feeling like a trapped mouse when his mother asked him to stay in and help her put up the curtains. He cheered up after the arrival of the guests and asked in an eager voice, "Do people get paid for writing in newspapers?"

"Of course they do," said Hemen, "this is a commercial newspaper so they are bound to pay a proper honorarium."

"Will Mom get it too?"

"Certainly."

Tatai's curiosity grew. He looked at his mother and then at the other two. "How much will she get?"

"Five or six hundred at least, if not more."

"Wow! Five or six hundred! Mom, this is going to be the first earning of your life, isn't it?"

Aditi smiled, looking delighted.

"One should never save one's first earning, you know. You should spend the whole of it."

Aditi continued to smile.

"I'm booking a Chinese meal in advance, Mom," said Tatai getting up from the sofa.

Everyone got talking in earnest once Tatai left the room. Hemen was here after a gap of nearly three weeks. When he came the last time the house had been full of guests. Supratim's brother Partha was there with Kaveri and Babai, plus both Supratim's sisters, their spouses and children. It was the last family gathering before Partha left for Lucknow. Aditi had hardly been able to speak to Hemen properly in that crowd.

Hemen appeared to be in real high spirits and kept Aditi and Ranjan amused with jokes and anecdotes from the lives of senior writers whom he had known personally. In between they argued on various themes, such as realism in literature, the meeting point of facts and fantasy, myths and their likenesses and differences with realism, the intimate relationship between theme and style and so on. Many new and interesting points came up as they argued. When at last Ranjan stood up to go Aditi asked him, "When will you come again?"

"Soon. One of these days."

"That's what you had told me the last time but it took you full three months to come again."

"How could he come before?" Hemen chipped in. "He was too busy working on his various commitments for the puja numbers. What all did you manage to write this time, Ranjan?"

"A few short stories, a novel and a trivial article," said Ranjan in a shy voice.

Aditi opened her eyes wide. So many things!

"Writing for the puja numbers is like an addiction for the upcoming writers," remarked Hemen, "You can't realise what it's like, Aditi. Writing for one, then another, and then yet another. I didn't bring out a special puja number this time but there are many others who did."

"You won't need to explain what it's like," said Ranjan, "She will realise it for herself in a year or two if she continues to write. When it happens she won't have the time to remember who has been visiting her and who hasn't during this period. Writing is such an addiction. More difficult to give up than drinks."

"Right," agreed Hemen. "Well Aditi, we could have the next literary meet at your place, couldn't we?"

"Here? That would be lovely! When would you like to have it? And how many people should I expect?"

"Oh quite a few. Ranjan, why don't you ask some people from your own literary group? And do ask Anisur to come."

"It would be like showing a broken fence to the fox," said Ranjan laughing. "Our group is full of nutty characters. If you give them the green signal they will land up in droves."

"I wouldn't mind that. At least my flat would be of some use to people."

"Then when should we make it?" asked Hemen.

"You tell me. What about the Sunday after the next?"

"Are you sure you won't be put to any inconvenience?"

"Quite sure."

Aditi was brimming over with excitement. A waterfall seemed to gush deep down within her heart, breaking up the stones and throwing aside the pebbles to make a path for itself. Her static and stagnant life seemed to come alive once again.

Supratim returned late that night. Some of the big bosses from Mumbai were here holding long meetings on sales and promotion. After the meeting they had all gone to the club for drinks and dinner. Supratim had downed quite a few pegs himself and was feeling on top of the world. He spoke nineteen to the dozen when he returned home.

"Do you know what Bhogle told me? He said, Mazumdar, you are a genius. Do you know why he said it?"

Aditi was dying to tell him about her story. Papai and Tatai were having dinner in the dining space. Aditi served them and came to the drawing room.

"Why?" she asked him, keeping her own news to herself.

Supratim slumped into the sofa sitting right beside Aditi. "Because no other zone has been able to reach our half-yearly target except mine. And it's not just the target either. Our new shampoo has proved to be a total flop everywhere else except in my zone. After all, Ranganath can't expect to have his own way every time! Do you know what he had done?"

This time Aditi couldn't stop herself from interrupting him. "You know, I have a wonderful piece of news too."

"You?"

"Yes, me."

"What is it?"

"My story, the one Hemen Mama had taken from me the last time, is going to appear in tomorrow's newspaper."

"Will it? Well, I thought it would be a piece of real news! From the way you said it, it seemed as though ..."

"As though what? Wouldn't you call this a piece of wonderful news?"

Supratim smiled at her, his eyes dreamy. "Do you know what I had thought from the way you said it?"

"What?"

Supratim looked at her sons, busy tucking in, and whispered, "That you were expecting our third after Papai and Tatai."

"How you love to tease!" Aditi couldn't help laughing. "Now tell me, isn't my news quite wonderful too?"

"Yes, it's quite good. It means you are gradually making a name for yourself. But you should also give me some credit for your success."

"Why?"

"Don't imagine that Hemen Mama has been the only one to encourage you. Haven't I been telling you all along to put your afternoons to some use instead of wasting your time? I have also said that writing is far better than remaining idle or getting into mischief."

Aditi shook her head absent-mindedly. "I suppose you did."

"Good that you remembered. Now, don't you ever forget it!"

Supratim took off his socks and shoved them inside his shoes.

"What was I saying?"

"About what?"

Supratim scratched his head for a while, thinking deeply.

"Oh yes, I remember. Ranganathan. Do you know what he had done? Something quite unimaginable! He sold detergents worth 42 lakhs to the railways. Do you know how he managed it?"

"How?" asked Aditi in a disinterested voice.

"Because he had high connections. His uncle-in-law was Member, Railway Board. He was the key figure in that transaction. Otherwise can you imagine the railways buying detergents? Mukherjee, our purchasing officer told me, well Mazumdar, why not send your boys to the garbage dump at Dhapa and get them to sell perfumes there? ha ha ha! Isn't that a good joke? And now Ranganathan is going to get it hot and strong. Ask me why. Go on, ask me..."

"Why?" asked Aditi taking another long breath.

"Because the CBI is now after the uncle-in-law. He is as good as dead meat. So, of course Ranganathan's order has been cancelled. He'll now be obliged to take to saffron robes and go a-begging in the streets of Chennai, crying

Give me an order
Give me an order
Give me an order,
For Almighty's sake!

ha ha ha!"

Supratim's loud song and laughter brought the two brothers pell mell from the dining space. Tatai sat beside him and put his feet up.

"Better ask Dad for a sitting like this every night, Mom. You will find several plots for your stories and your income will rise in leaps and bounds."

"Income? Are you going to be paid for your writing?"

"Naturally, if I write for newspapers," said Aditi with the ghost of a smile.

"A minimum of five or six hundred for each story," Tatai added.

Supratim looked surprised. "Not bad! Not bad at all!" he said. "However small the amount might be, money is money after all! Of course you could have made much more if you had stuck to your sari business. But you might argue that this doesn't need any investment except for paper, pen and ink. Very well, I shall supply the plots and you can write away." Supratim broke into a loud guffaw.

Papai hardly spoke to anyone at home these days unless there was real need. Neither with Aditi nor Supratim nor with Tatai. A fortnight remained for his GRE tests. The results of his B Sc finals were expected to be out within a month. He looked worried whenever he stayed at home. But even he couldn't stop himself from saying, "Don't look down on writers. Even writers manage to make millions these days. You hear about so many writers abroad who have built regular palaces, bought islands and airplanes and what not by their writing."

His unexpected comment led to a fresh round of discussions. The talk turned to which writers earned the most, who had the most expensive lifestyle, which ones were sold on drinks, which ones were on drugs and which were womanizers and so it went on and on with little bearing on actual facts. Aditi felt hurt and mortified. Here were all three in her family discussing writers and yet not one of them had bothered to ask her which of her stories was going to be published the next day. All three were concerned about money, just how much money each writer made. Were these really Aditi's own husband and sons?

Just look at Papai. He was not the least bit repentant about his affairs and behaved as though Aditi had been in the wrong all along for having intruded into his private life. Even now he continued to bill and coo unabashed into the mouth piece regularly. With a number of different girls, no doubt. Aditi had tried her best to forgive him. But the hurt still pricked her like a thorn. It is easy enough for a mother to forgive her child but it is painfully difficult to forget the action itself. As for Tatai, her happy go lucky, jovial younger son, he was nothing if not a baniya, his world centering around money. Otherwise how could anyone so young find so much interest in share markets? Aditi was about to go into the bedroom when she suddenly turned back and spoke to Supratim.

"I forgot to tell you something important. I have called for a literary meet at our place the Sunday after next."

"Here? That too on a Sunday, my only free day?"

"It's for just one day. Can't you put up with it for once?"

Supratim looked at Aditi. What he read in her face prompted him to say, "Oh very well. Have it your way. But there's a slight problem."

"What is it?"

"Tathagata said he might drop in the same Sunday."

"Ask him to come the Sunday after. Oh yes, one more thing. I'd like to ask Hemen Mama and Ranjan for lunch that Sunday."

"Why?"

"Because I want to."

Aditi did not wait for a reply. A sense of utter loneliness seemed to surround her from all sides. She woke up very early the next morning. The entire house was still asleep when she tiptoed out of the room. It was still too early for the newspaper man. But before he arrived Aditi wanted to touch her story with her hands. All by herself.

Chapter Fourteen

It had been autumn when Aditi had first brought the parrot home. It was now autumn once again. With it had come a wonderful transformation in the bird. It was beginning to talk. Not many words. Truthfully speaking, its current vocabulary comprised a single word, Khuku. It had not learnt to whistle. Nor could it say anything else. Just Khuku. It repeated the word over and over again, morning , noon and evening. Khuku, Khuku, Khuku!

Everyone in the house was tired of hearing it.

Everyone except Aditi.

To her it was a distinct proof that the bird was not dumb. What else did one expect from a parrot?

It was getting stronger by the day. It flapped its wings loudly, shaking the entire cage. Looking at it now one could hardly locate which of its wings had been hurt or where the tomcat had pawed it so mercilessly.

Aditi no longer had any time for the parrot. In fact she had little time for anything except her writing these days. Something that had been a mere hobby or pastime even a few months ago was now her whole world. Something to strive for, look forward to. It took up a great deal of her time, not just the afternoons. And she refused to be interrupted. If neighbours or relatives dropped in while she was writing she answered them absent-mindedly and was curt and aloof. She glibly told Papai and Tatai to find things for themselves instead of doing everything for them. She asked them to help themselves when they wanted anything. Evening was the only time when she didn't write and made time for her family. She turned to writing again when it was night. Not quite every night perhaps, but most of the nights. Because there was little chance of being disturbed at that hour and it helped her concentrate better.

But such a state of affairs did not last for long. Supratim woke up one night when it was nearly midnight. The light was on. Aditi lay rolling on the floor, the pillow tucked under her, writing away. Supratim looked at her and rubbed his sleepy eyes.

"What do you think you're doing? Won't you even let a fellow sleep in peace?"

"I started writing after you fell asleep," protested Aditi.

"Must you really write at midnight?"

Aditi smiled. "I can't help it. All kinds of fresh ideas come crowding into my mind when it's night. I seem to visualize so many new things when I am by the window and remember so many forgotten incidents. All of it helps me write better, you know."

Supratim made a face. "Keep collecting ideas and incidents to your heart's content during the day. There's no one to disturb you or stop you from doing it."

"But the pictures vanish when it's day and I can't seem to find them again."

"So I must be obliged to forgo my hard earned sleep while you hunt for pictures," grumbled Supratim, "You know jolly well that I can't sleep with the lights on. I come home dog tired after a hard day's work. It's darn unfair if I am not allowed even a little sleep at night."

Aditi could have reminded him that there had been many, many nights in the last 24 years when Supratim had kept the lights on at night completing his office work, despite knowing full well that Aditi could not sleep with lights on either. But he had never bothered to switch off the lights for her sake even when he might have done. Even now he often watched late night movies with the boys. In fact they had been watching a football match on TV until three in the morning only last week. Aditi had not complained that the light and the sound had kept her awake all night. Didn't she deserve a good night's sleep like everyone else? But Aditi did not give voice to her thoughts. She put away her papers quietly, switched off the light and got back to bed. But she bought herself a table lamp the very next day. She'd have to get over her habit of rolling on the floor when writing, she told herself.

Supratim laughed at first when he saw her writing with the table lamp on.

"You seem quite determined to become a Nobel Laureate or something," he said in a teasing voice.

After a few nights he blurted out, "I really call this going too far."

"Why? Does even the table lamp keep you awake?"

"It's not a question of my keeping awake or not. I feel there should be a limit to everything. You are crossing that limit. You don't have to earn your livelihood with your pen. Then why do you need to write so desperately, to the exclusion of everything else? I hate to see you slogging away like this!"

"Do you mean to say that crossing limits is justified only when there's a question of earning one's livelihood?"

Supratim said no more. But he continued to look glum.

For the first time in her life Aditi had taken to serious study. She was really eager to find out all about the big wide world outside. The subject was of secondary importance. She eagerly devoured stories, novels, books on art, culture, history and anything else Hemen Mama gave her to read. She became a member of the Ramakrishna Mission library at Gol Park, picking up several books from there as well. Ranjan kept her well supplied with any number of little magazines and mini magazines. She found them equally fascinating.

Aditi now held regular literary meets in her house where many young writers dropped in regularly. Hemen and Ranjan were the main organisers of the meets. Stories were read, followed by discussions and debates. Aditi's dining space turned into a full fledged lecture hall at the time. Her entire flat rang with the sound of eager voices until late at night. Aditi had already made several trips to the meets held at Premtosh's place along with Hemen. But the meets organised at her place were less formal and therefore far more popular. At the formal meets at Premtosh's place most of the people were listeners. At Aditi's, everyone was a speaker, discussing varied issues with eagerness and ease.

The young writers who were regulars at her place were of many kinds. Some were unduly serious and reserved. Others spoke non-stop like sizzling fireworks. Some were exceedingly shy, barely managing to read out their stories in shaky, bashful voices and waited with bent heads for the comments from others. Some barked like wild dogs at the slightest criticism of their work. Aditi never failed to feel a kind of warmth from their presence. The warmth of a fellow writer and fellow thinker. It was impossible to remain stiff and formal amidst so many young and enthusiastic people. Aditi had become quite adept at expressing her opinion freely.

The first literary meet organised at her place had been a special affair. She had gone for an elaborate menu comprising hot luchis, dum aloo, vegetable cutlets and dessert accompanied by several rounds of tea. She had made the tea and fried the luchis herself.

Hemen cornered her the moment the others had left.

"Are you going to make such elaborate arrangements every time we have a meet at your place?"

"Oh well," said Aditi, "I had invited them after all..."

"Yes, but it was an invitation to speak and discuss, not an invitation to dinner. Please don't do it again."

Aditi's face fell. She had greatly enjoyed feeding the group of eager, enthusiastic youngsters. Why did Hemen mind her doing it?

"Shall I serve nothing at all the next time?" she asked meekly.

"I didn't say that. Serve tea, by all means. Several rounds if you like. Tea with puffed rice and fried peanuts. They go very well with literary discussions. Why not ask your boys to help make the tea?"

Aditi had merely laughed. It was highly unlikely that either of them would be anywhere around to help her. Both tended to run in the opposite direction if they so much as heard the word literature. To both it was something utterly, exceedingly boring! Papai's GRE exams were complete. His BSc results were out. He had graduated with first class honours and had taken admission in the university for his Master's degree. But his heart was concerned with his GRE alone. Aditi was reconciled to the idea by now.

What was really surprising was that Supratim had been present at her first literary meet, either because Aditi had specially requested him to be there or because of sheer curiosity. But his presence caused problems on all fronts, for Aditi herself as well as him. In his eagerness to play host Supratim got talking to a young writer with soft looks. Supratim spoke to him in a rather patronising manner which turned out to be his undoing. The writer suddenly asked him, "You hold a very high profile job, don't you?"

Supratim laughed. "So you've found that out as well, eh? Who told you?"

"I heard Hemenbabu mention it. You are the head of Lotus India for the entire eastern zone, aren't you?"

"Nothing as grand as that. I merely look after the sales."

"Your company spends a great deal on advertisements. Why don't you give one for our magazine as well?"

Aditi, who was sitting beside Supratim, heard him and added her plea. "Yes, why don't you?"

"Well, I guess something can be arranged. What's the name of your magazine?"

"Rohini."

"What are the sales figures like?"

"Good. Pretty good. We printed 400 copies of our last issue out of which just about 60 remained unsold. There were about 40 complementary copies. Which means nearly 300 copies sold?"

Supratim looked taken aback. "Only 300 copies?"

"So what? It's not a very small number. At least we sold enough to recover the costs."

"What about the actual cost of printing?"

"Partly recovered from the ads that came in. The rest from our pockets, of course."

"Which proves you have enough means to afford the luxury of running a magazine," said Supratim laughing loudly.

"I wouldn't have asked for an ad had that been so. What I earn from my tuitions is not enough to bring out all the issues in time."

Supratim stared at him incredulously. "Don't you have a regular job?"

"I wouldn't have worried about my magazine if I did. I could have made it so much better and bigger."

"Is that your only reason for needing a job? To bring out a bigger magazine?"

The writer was perfectly honest.

"A job would be of no use to me unless it helped me bring out my magazine just the way I'd like to."

"Don't you have a family to look after? Parents or any one else?"

"Of course I have. Parents, brother and sisters. But why do you ask? What has my family got to do with it?"

Supratim could not think of a suitable answer. He sat staring at the group for a while and finally got up and strode out of the room.

"Your satellites are a pack of loonies," he told Aditi that night after everyone had left.

Aditi gave him a crooked smile. "Why? Just because he asked you for an advertisement?"

"Advertisement for a magazine that sells just 300 copies! It's downright absurd! Money doesn't grow on trees!"

"You don't mind spending lakhs when it comes to vulgar song and dance sequences on the TV and yet you blow your top at the thought of parting with a meagre hundred or two hundred for a genuine cause. At least the boys are trying to do something creative."

"Creative, my foot! It's sheer madness and selfishness if you ask me, to have no concern for one's family and blow up every bit of one's earning bringing out a stupid magazine! Utter rot!"

"Everyone is not cast in the same mould as you. Nor does everyone consider earning money to be the be-all and end-all of existence."

"Don't lecture me, for goodness' sake, and don't you ever involve me again in your stupid, worthless affairs!"

That had been the end of it all. Supratim refused point blank to attend any more of the meets organised by her. He made for Agartala during the second one. During the third he left the house the minute the first guest rang the door bell and returned around midnight, dead drunk – something he rarely did as a rule.

He yelled his head off the moment he stepped into the house.

"Has your brood of worthless buggers left or not?"

Aditi was stunned at first. Then she too shouted back at him.

"What do you think you are doing, returning at midnight and waking up the entire neighbourhood?"

"I have every right to do what I please in my own house. Where are all those sons of a bitch?"

"Mind your language! Are you aware of what the word means?"

"Oh no, I don't! I have to learn everything from you afresh," screamed Supratim throwing the shoes on the door. Then he tottered into the bedroom, muttering, "To hell with language! Making my life an absolute hell!"

Aditi tried to quieten him.

"Why are you so mad about my literary meets? I hold it just one evening in the whole month."

"But why should I put up with even that? Why should a pack of busybodies who have no business to be here let their hair down in my flat? Even one day a month? Is it a joke, eh?"

Aditi banged the door shut. "Will you shut up? You will wake up Papai and Tatai."

"Let them wake up! Let the whole world see what you have been up to!"

Supratim flung the door open with tottering steps.

"Here you, Papai and Tatai, you tell me, is this joke? Can a body expect to put up with such doings any longer?"

Aditi dragged Supratim to the bed and forced him to sit down.

"You are mad because my friends have been visiting me here, isn't it? What about the times when your friends come here and let their hair down? You don't seem to mind it!"

Supratim hissed. "Don't you dare to compare my friends to your pack of loafers and beggars! And that old lecher of an uncle who has been turning your head until you are unable to see straight! Why is he so keen to turn you into a writer, you tell me that! What business is it of his? Just so that he can keep shoving in cartloads of young men into my flat? Just so he can find an excuse for taking you out goodness knows where whenever he feels like it? Do you think I don't understand what all this means?"

Aditi had turned into a statue. She felt as though a wild cat was scratching right across her heart making her entire body wrench in pain. But her words were clear and distinct as she said,

"I don't know if you realise what you have been blabbering in your drunken state but you better understand once and for all that my friends will continue to come here. So will my uncle. This flat is as much mine as yours."

"Is it? Please remember, your father or brother did not gift it to you in a will. I bought it with my own hard earned money."

"But haven't I also given you the best part of my life, running your home and looking after your children? Does that give me no right to the place?"

"Shut up and don't talk rubbish. Who says you have worked for nothing? I have given you every blessed thing you asked for!" Supratim's words were blurred. "But I won't allow all this under my roof any more. I do hereby declare ....."

Aditi hung down her head. Then she whispered in a voice almost inaudible, "So this is what you have really felt all along? These are your actual feelings, what you are now telling me?"

"Yes, it is! I could have told you all this much sooner. I didn't out of pity, because I wanted to give you a chance. I thought it would be no more than a harmless pastime, since you had nothing better to do. But I have had more than I can stand. Put an end to it, for goodness' sake. This is my house. It's supposed to be an abode of peace and happiness. I won't allow a pack of brats to ruin it."

Aditi had reached the very limit of her tolerance. Was it mere drunken chatter or was Supratim really spilling out what lay buried deep down in his heart? His actual feelings?

Aditi felt an earthquake far down below shatter her inner world. The massive palace she had built with an effort of 24 long years crumbled like a sand castle. So did the faith, that it was she who had been the life force behind it. Aditi held her breath and whispered, "Very well. It shall be as you wish from now on."

The winter night seemed to be made of layers of ice that froze both body and soul. The distant hills sent down a chilling breeze of frozen anguish. The bird was curled up, trying to find warmth in the severe cold. Aditi's entire being seemed frozen. Supratim muttered himself to sleep, one leg hanging out of the bed. Aditi picked it up and tucked the quilt around Supratim and went on to put the mosquito net down. She picked up Supratim's shawl from the floor, folded it up neatly and kept it inside the wardrobe. Then she switched off the light and sat at her writing table. After sitting quietly for a while she switched on the table lamp. Her part of the room glowed brightly under the light. Then she switched off the light again letting the room get dark once again. She sat there for a long time switching the table lamp off and on, a million questions humming within her heart like a swarm of bees. A million questions!

Chapter Fifteen

Aditi had been to visit Rina, her younger sister in law. Rina had called up several times during the last few days telling them how worried she was about her elder daughter's illness. It would look really odd if she didn't go to see how she was doing after hearing all about it. On reaching there Aditi found that the fever had come down but the girl still suffered from a terrible cough. The doctor was almost certain that it was only a severe case of bronchitis. But he had asked them to get an X-ray done just to be on the safe side. Rina's husband was supposed to collect the X-ray report on his way back from the office. So he was late returning home, having gone to the doctor with the report first. Fortunately the report made it clear that it was a simple case of bronchitis. So the doctor had merely prescribed a cough syrup. Aditi waited until her brother-in-law's return so as to learn first hand what the doctor had said. It was well past nine by the time she reached home. Supratim had already returned. He sat watching an action film on TV, his feet up on the centre table, the shawl wrapped around him. He looked at Aditi and asked, "How is Rinkie?"

Aditi had turned extremely quiet of late. Her heart felt like a load of ashes since that fateful night but she did not choose to wear her heart on her sleeves. Outwardly she appeared to live just the way she had always done, doing whatever needed to be seen to, looking after the house and its inmates as usual. On two afternoons she had even sat down to write. But she refused to speak unless spoken to. Not that anyone noticed, especially her sons. They neither had the eyes nor the time to see if their mother had changed. Both went out and came in as they pleased, tucked into the food as usual, went to sleep when they felt like and ordered Aditi about to do this or that the way they had always done. Neither did Supratim appear to be particularly repentant for what he had said and done that night. He behaved as though the drunken scene hadn't actually happened.

Winter seemed to be getting more severe by the day. It was painful to walk on the floor on bare feet. Aditi took off her shoes and got into her slippers. She looked at Supratim.

"Rinki is better except for a bad cough."

"Anything serious?"

"No."

Supratim tapped his feet on the table. "A piece of wonderful news here."

Aditi did not show any interest or ask any questions.

Supratim spoke up on his own. "The GRE results are out. Your son has done brilliantly. He has just taken his friends out to a late night movie to celebrate."

"Is that so?" Aditi did not sound particularly thrilled.

"I don't understand the intricacies of the exam myself, but Papai said he has managed to get an excellent score. So there is every chance of his being able to get into a good university in the States."

"Good," said Aditi and went in to change her sari.

Tatai was at home. Aditi served dinner and called father and son. All three sat down to eat.

"I've been thinking of something," said Supratim dipping his chapati in the bowl of cauliflower-and-potato curry.

"What?"

"You had been asking me to get the flat colour-washed for a long time. I couldn't manage it last year. Shall I get it done this year?"

"If you like."

"What colour should we choose?"

"Beige, please have it colour washed beige," cried Tatai enthusiastically.

Supratim frowned. "What sort of colour is that?"

"Something between sandalwood and brown. You'll know the exact shade when you see the shade card."

Supratim looked at Aditi through the corner of his eye.

"No, it shall be the colour your mother chooses."

"I know Mom likes beige very much, don't you, Mom?"

"Whatever you choose is fine with me," said Aditi straining at the casserole, "More chapatis?"

"Just one."

"Shall I call the contractor tomorrow and ask him to give me an estimate?" asked Supratim.

Aditi nodded silently.

Supratim looked at Aditi once again.

"You know, Tatai, I have been thinking of something else as well."

"What is it?"

"Don't you remember your brother telling me once that if your mother continued to write seriously I should get her stories published as a book? Now that she has had so many published I think it would be a good idea to get them into a book. What do you say? Wouldn't that be nice?"

Clever Tatai took in the situation at a glance and smiled to himself. Then he looked at both his parents.

"A fab idea," he said.

"Well, you are often in College Street. Why don't you find out for me how much it is likely to cost?"

"Is there enough salt in the curry?" Aditi asked in a dispassionate voice, "Sabita tends to tip in a little too much these days."

Supratim seemed to get a jolt. He stopped talking and finished the rest of his meal in glum silence and left the place soon after.

Everyone went to bed late that night. Aditi heated up Papai's dinner after he returned home from the movie show. Papai sounded unduly elated about his GRE results and Aditi smiled in acknowledgement. A small, measured smile.

Supratim was in bed, well tucked inside the quilt when Aditi got in.

"What on earth is the matter with you?" he asked Aditi as she switched off the light.

"Nothing," she answered in a casual voice.

"Phool, do you intend to remain eternally mad with me for something I blurted out in a drunken state?"

"Do I appear to be mad?"

"Then why aren't you happy despite my two thrilling plans for you?"

"Which do you mean? Getting the house colour washed or getting my stories published as a book?"

Supratim didn't answer. His silence appeared to enhance the darkness, making it seem bottomless. A pitch-like darkness , thick and dense. Supratim moved his hand and touched Aditi.

"Look here, Phool, we have been married for nearly 25 years now. You are no longer a blushing bride and I am no longer a nervous, jittery groom. Should we play useless games of misunderstanding at this stage of our life? Don't we know each other like the back of our hands?"

Aditi did not reply.

Supratim came closer. "Yes, we have had our share of small misunderstandings. That's only natural. But for all that, you know how much I love you and I know how much you love me. None of us really want to hurt the other, do we?"

Was there a note of uncertainty in Supratim's voice? Otherwise why did he need to spell out his love in so many words after 24 long years of marriage?

"Let's change the subject," said Aditi firmly.

"Why should I change it? I need to speak out." Supratim coughed and cleared his throat. "I am sure you realise that whatever I have done is for your own good. If I feel that you are going astray, I shall certainly try to stop you. And if you feel that I am doing anything wrong you have every right to stop me too. I pulled myself away the minute you told me that you didn't like my being involved in Deepak and Sharmila's private life. They are divorced now and Sharmila has the custody of their son. But I haven't butted into their affairs again, have I? I told Deepak quite frankly and clearly that I can't get involved in his affairs any more because my wife does not like it. Ask Deepak yourself if you don't believe me. We have such a nice and cosy, well-knitted family with you and me and our two bright and intelligent sons. We shall soon be celebrating our silver wedding in our newly done-up flat. Why should we let any outsider ruin our family peace?

Aditi smiled in the darkness. A sad, pathetic smile that matched the coldness of the room.

Supratim took Aditi in his arms and whispered, "I shall tell you something if you promise not to be angry with me."

"What is it?"

"Your Hemen Mama was here this evening. I have explained to him very nicely and politely that you are, after all, a married lady with commitments and duties of your own, so it is not possible for you to be involved in literary activities in the same way as him. The situations are very different."

Aditi could not keep silent any longer. She sat up in bed throwing off her quilt.

"When had he come?"

"In the evening. He wanted to take you to Barasat or some such place the next week. But I have told him that you cannot go. I wasn't rude or ill-mannered. I spoke to him very gently and politely. Tatai was there too. Ask him if you don't believe me."

Supratim did not sound hesitant or repentant as he spoke his mind.

"You do have a talent which he was the first to discover. We are all grateful to him for that. But now that we too know about it we also know how to treat it with due respect. Don't we all keep telling people how talented you are? But why allow your talent to upset your home life? Women need to be a little reserved and maintain a discreet distance from outsiders. It only enables people to give her the respect that is her due. And it strengthens the foundations of married life. Hemen Mama is a bachelor himself. That is why he hasn't the foggiest notion as to how a married woman ought to behave. Perhaps you hadn't thought of it this way. But I feel quite sure that you don't wish to ruin your family and home for the sake of your writing. Or do you?"

The night air froze outside. Aditi sat like a statue without her quilt. She did not feel the cold. She had turned to ice herself.

Chapter Sixteen

The house had the look of a nightmare. There was no dearth of ancient, tumble-down buildings in this part of the city. But this building certainly beat them to flinders. It was not merely shoddy and ramshackle. It was a virtual ruin. The coating of cement had fallen off decades ago. The entire wall was a maze of cracks. A few reddish bricks stuck out here and there like raw wounds. It was obvious that the place had been left to its fate without so much as a minor repair for at least fifty years, if not more. Peepal and banyan trees had dug in their roots through the bigger cracks. The saplings clung to the moss covered wall like huddled up midgets. So this is where Hemen Mama lived!

The main door of the building made of thick wood stood open. Aditi hesitated for a moment and rattled the big iron ring on the door. No one appeared to have heard it. The square courtyard inside, once made of stone, was covered with a thick layer of green moss. Despite being mid afternoon, the whole place looked dark, damp and gloomy. A huge reservoir stood in a corner of the courtyard that had a narrow veranda running along its sides, with a series of openings, meant to be doors. The sound of a female voice wafted out of one of them followed by total silence. A child whined somewhere indoors, followed by somebody scolding.

Aditi felt impatient. Why didn't someone come out at least? Had she managed to land up at the wrong house? Perhaps she ought to have taken better directions from her uncle when she had asked for Hemen Mama's address. But there seemed little chance of her having made a mistake. This must indeed be the place Hemen Mama had spoken of. After getting down at Hati Bagan, proceeding towards the Central Avenue along the left footpath, the first turning to the left, the second lane to the right and the fifth house on that lane. This was the place.

A feeling of deep resentment had driven Aditi to find this place. But why had she come? To ask for Hemen Mama's forgiveness on Supratim's behalf? And would everything be hunky dory once again if Hemen did forgive him? Could a mere apology justify Supratim's unpardonable behaviour? Should Aditi break into tears before Hemen Mama? But wouldn't that reek too much of melodrama? Should she go back home despite having taken the trouble to come all this way?

Aditi rattled the ring once again, this time louder than the last. Someone answered it at last. A middle aged woman, fat and discoloured like dry grass, came out and said with a disgruntled expression, "No, no, we don't want any of your stuff. You may as well make yourself scarce right away."

Aditi was taken aback at the woman's mistaking her for a salesgirl. She was wearing an expensive off-white sari with a black and gold border, a Kashmiri shawl and carried a classy handbag, not a tote bag. Nor was she carrying any ware! How could she possibly mistake her for a salesgirl?

"I am not a salesgirl. I have come to find out something important," she told the woman in a desperate voice.

The woman didn't seem to hear her. Turning her back to Aditi she pulled down the sari that was drying on the line, smelt it and dumped it on her shoulder. Then she turned to Aditi once more.

"What are you waiting for? Didn't I tell you that we don't need any of your stuff?"

Before Aditi could think of a reply a young girl ran out from the room on the opposite side. She looked the same age as Tultuli and had the look of a colourful butterfly. She seemed to be in a great hurry as she slipped on her wrist watch and came dashing out to Aditi.

"What have you got there? Come on, show it quick."

"I am looking for someone. Can you help me?" Aditi asked in a serious voice.

"Is that so?" The girl looked disappointed. "Who are you looking for?"

"Hemendra Narayan Mullick, the editor of *Bahta* magazine. Does he live here?"

The girl looked startled. Then she stared at Aditi. "Are you really looking for grand uncle?"

Aditi heaved a sigh of relief. So she had not landed up at the wrong address.

The girl pointed to the old woman.

"Didn't she tell you where he is?"

Aditi frowned. "No, she didn't. I wonder why."

"That's her way, I guess. The other day a friend of mine had come looking for him and had to go back without her telling my friend a word about him."

Had it been any other time Aditi might have found the episode amusing and laughed right out. She merely said, "Could you tell me if Hemen Mama is in?"

"Is he really your uncle?"

"Yes, he is. Is he at home?"

"Goodness knows. It's difficult for people to know when he is in or when he is out."

She thought for a moment and said, "You could do something. Go up the stairs to the first floor and try the fourth door. If you find it locked, he is obviously not in."

The stairs were steep and broken. The railing was shaky and tottering. Aditi went up the steps carefully. She remembered her uncle remarking, 'Hemen's house is the outside of enough.' He had been perfectly right. Going up the steps really made her head reel. Her uncle must have meant the same staircase when he said it. Her heart grew cold at the sight of the fourth door. A big lock hung on the door clasp. She stood still before the locked door not knowing what to do next.

The door next to it opened suddenly. An old woman stood there staring at Aditi.

"Does Hemen Mama live here?" Aditi asked stammering with hesitation.

The old woman grimaced showing a toothless jaw. "What mama?"

"I meant Hemen Mullick."

"I see! So he has started acquiring nieces now, has he? It used to be brothers young enough to be his sons before!"

The old woman gave her a distasteful look. "He is not here, as you can see."

"When will he be back?" Aditi's voice was stern too.

The woman looked her up and down as she said, "Can't say. Never bothers to tell us his whereabouts."

"Can you give him a message? Please tell him that Aditi Mazumdar from Selimpur had come to see him."

"No I can't. Write your message on a slip of paper and push it under his door."

"You live right next door and you appear to be related to

him. Can't you even give him a simple message?" Aditi asked in an angry voice.

The old woman erupted like a volcano.

"Why should I? Just because I happen to live next door? I tell you, he doesn't belong to our family! When he first returned home after his retirement, we were all so nice to him. I had told him, 'Have your meals with us and pay us what you can from your pension money.' But would he listen? Threw up a fit and started having his meals in a hotel after barely two months. Why should I bother to keep in touch with such a relative? All he ever does is scribble loads of rubbish and that too not for himself. I hear he's taken to bringing out some newspaper for someone else. That's how he has been blowing up his money and we are expected to hold our tongues about it! Even if he imagines himself to be a Tagore or Bankim, he has been wasting hard cash on people who don't even belong to the family! Do you expect me to put up with such outlandish behaviour? Here are we, barely able to fit ourselves in, and the wretch has been occupying an entire room, piling up his rubbish. Two of my nephews are simply lying in wait. Said they are going to grab the room the moment he kicks the bucket. But my son has warned them that he won't allow it. After all, his youngest uncle's room should rightfully belong to him after he dies."

Aditi climbed down the stairs feeling totally exhausted all of a sudden. So this is where Hemen Mama lived. In an environment as ghastly as this! And yet, there was a constant smile on his lips, whenever Aditi met him. She had known that he lived alone. But a loneliness of this degree, with not a soul to call his own despite a house full of relatives! And this was the man whom Supratim had insulted so glibly. Hemen had once told her, 'I don't have the intensity of feeling which a writer needs to have, Aditi. Whatever I write sounds insipid.'

What did intensity of feelings imply? Wasn't his life, totally devoted to the finding and making of new writers, intense enough? How else could one describe this totally selfless craving?

The winter afternoon melted into evening. An icy wind whipped across the land. The sun grew weak and dusky, about to disappear as Aditi traced her way back home. A totally different Aditi.

Chapter Seventeen

"Dear Hemen Mama,

This is my first letter to you and probably my last.

I am not writing to you today to justify Supratim's actions or words. What Supratim says or does is his own responsibility, not mine. This letter is entirely about myself.

You had appeared in my life like a meteorite. I had been happy enough in my past existence, half awake and half asleep. Your sudden appearance turned my placid world upside down. Why did you shake up my entire existence, Hemen Mama, and force me to think for myself for the first time in my life?

An ordinary woman like me is destined to live according to a set pattern laid down by the society. The way thousands of women have done before me, from the beginning of time. To look after one's home, husband and children until one finds oneself alone, quietly waiting for death. That is what I too would have done. My entire existence had once centred around my home, my husband and sons. I did it because I thought that was what I was meant to do. Because that was the way of the world, of what life was all about. I knew it to be my destiny.

Why did you make me realise that something more remains in a woman's life, even after she has done her duty by her husband, children and home? Why did you force me to see that even I was capable of doing something more, if I tried? It is because of you that I learnt to think of myself as a complete human being. Someone who can see and think for herself and express it in her own words. What folly! What utter foolishness on my part! When a man follows his star to become a writer or an artist and turns Bohemian as a result it is considered a part of his artistic expression. But a woman always has to remain within the bounds chalked out by the society, whether she wants to write or paint. She has to keep within the four walls of her home. No one is going to put up with it if she dares to move out even a single step. Why did you make me forget these harsh realities of life...albeit for just a few days? Supratim is a total man. So he pulled me back on track in time, making me see clearly wherein lies my limit.

A question troubles me all day long to which I crave to find an answer. Who is Aditi? The wife of Supratim Mazumdar? The mother of Papai and Tatai? Was she born just to fulfil the needs of the three? Doesn't Aditi have any existence of her own? An existence meant just for herself?

My time is long past, Hemen Mama. One cannot do at fifty what one ought to have done at five. If one tries to do it by force it merely gives rise to complications which a woman of my years can neither face nor get over. My afternoons will arrive and simply melt into evening. Quietly and uneventfully.

My friend Sujata says, married life is like tightrope walking. The old woman who lives in the flat opposite mine stands in the balcony all day, to drink in the scent of sunlight and air. It's all she is able to do. Another lady who lives in the next flat whispers scandals about other inmates the moment she gets a chance to open her mouth because she has nothing better to do. Bless me that I too might be able to live the same meaningless, flat existence like the other women around me.

I shall not take up my pen to write any more, Hemen Mama. It is my destiny to live my life in my own home with people who have now become total strangers. Please stay away from us. And be happy!"

There was a sound in the passage. Aditi listened carefully. The parrot was awake. It was unusually early for it to be up. Supratim was fast asleep, well wrapped up in his warm quilt. He was especially fond of this early morning sleep during winters. Aditi switched off the table lamp and came out of the room closing the door behind her. A beam of the early morning sun fell across the wall of the balcony. The parrot was gazing hungrily at the light, screeching softly. Strangely enough Aditi felt no affection for the bird. She wrapped a shawl about herself and carried the cage out to the balcony. The clear winter morning was bright and crisp with no trace of fog. A faint moon was still visible in a corner of the sky, looking pale and sick like a consumptive patient. The earth was still curled up in the intense cold. Aditi looked at the parrot and smiled.

"Well?" she asked, "Do you feel like flying?"

Squeak, squeak! Replied the bird.

"Are your wings strong enough? Do you really feel you can manage it?"

The parrot danced a little jig on its perch. Squeak, squeak! It cried again.

Aditi opened the door of the cage and brought out the bird, feeling its warm body against herself.

The parrot said, "Khuku! Khuku!"

Aditi looked at it with wild, unseeing eyes. "Khuku is dead!" she muttered, "You'd better die too!"

She threw the bird outside the grill.

It began to fall down as it fluttered its wings wildly and then it suddenly found its balance and managed to keep afloat in the air, making it finally to the railing of one of the houses.

Aditi bit her lips and muttered, "May the cats gobble you up."

Did her words reach the bird? It left the railing and flew off to the terrace of the next building and then, on to the TV antenna.

It turned its head and looked at Aditi before flying off to the Gulmohor tree. It flew again from there, across the sky until it was out of sight.

Aditi felt a shiver of excitement. So the bird, captive for so long, had really managed to fly away across the open sky despite its weak wings?

Was it because of its own innate ability? Or was it because of the irresistible call of freedom?

Aditi rushed indoors and picked up her letter from the table. Then she came out to the balcony again. She tore up the letter into shreds and let the tiny pieces float away in the air.

A single Aditi was now reduced to a million Aditis.... all of them floating away in the air.

Floating.... floating far, far away!

Glossary

Baba:	father
Bhai phota:	a special festival for brothers celebrated by the sisters
Bijoya:	the concluding celebrations of Durga puja, the main festival of Bengal.
Biriyani:	a rice dish cooked with meat
Bindi:	a dot worn on the forehead
Boudi:	sister-in-law (elder brother's wife)
Chappal:	slippers
Chunni:	a scarf worn with salwar and kurta
Dada:	elder brother
Dhoti:	unstitched cloth, usually white, worn by men
Didi:	elder sister
Kaviraj:	a doctor practising Ayurveda or the Indian School of Medicine
Khadi:	handloom woven cloth
Lakh:	one hundred thousand
Luchi:	a popular fried snack in Bengal
Navratan pulao:	a colourful fried rice
Pallu:	the free end of the sari
Pishi:	aunt (father's sister)
Roti:	thinly rolled-out bread, baked directly on the fire